Betty

Joyce Bennett-Hall

Published by

ISBN: 0692055258
ISBN-13: 978-0692055250

Dedication

This book is dedicated to my Mastermind partners:
Nicki Coble, Martha Mutz, and Angela Overby.

To my prayer partner, Kathryn Hack.

To Linda Rhoho who fielded the story for me.

To Dr. James Mellon who inspired me to stretch beyond my reach.

To my husband, Shawn Hall, who gave me the space to write this story.

CHAPTER 1

Betty

Oh dear God, help me. I'm scared to death. Really, really scared. I can't believe it's chasing me. Actually, chasing me. Are black snakes poisonous? I can't remember. Oh, I wish I'd paid more attention when we were studyin' snakes. Mr. Snake, please don't bite me. What was it that daddy said? Snakes can't make a quick turn. I got to find me a big rock. Ah, there's one. Can I make it? Feet don't let me down. Run faster Betty. Okay, here I go round and round. I'm gettin' dizzy. Now, I just have to find a spot where I can jump to the side. Here goes! Wow, daddy was right. Look at that snake go. It can't stop. I'm gettin' out of here before it does.

Why is it always me that has to get the water? Fergus is older and stronger. That snake scared the daylights out of me. I just about peed my pants. In fact, I think I did. I wish I could run home screaming. Can't because I'll get whipped if I spill the water. Oh, why is the creek so far?

Betty Malone is the second oldest of six children, three boys and three girls. She's considered tall for her age, around five foot five, with a slender build. Her shoulder-length red hair compliments her fair skin, which is sprinkled with freckles on her face. Fergus is 18 years old and the oldest boy. Betty is 16 and the oldest of the girls. Most of the heavy chores fall on them. Then there's Kate, 14, who has the responsibility of the chickens, hen house, and collecting the eggs. Albert is ten. Howie is nine and the youngest is four-year-old Rose.

Betty, struggling with the heavy pail of water, headed back to the family's cabin. She was still experiencing the effects of being scared. Her hands were shaking and she felt a bit sick to her stomach. All the way home she kept looking over her shoulder for any more snakes. By the time she got to the door of the cabin, as hard as she tried not to, she had spilled some of the water.

"Well, it's about time you got back with that water," Margaret, Betty's mom, said with annoyance.

"A snake started to chase-" Margaret cut off Betty before she could finish her story.

"Hush Betty, with that nonsense. Go and see what's keepin' your brother with that firewood. Kate, put the eggs on the table and when you're done, get Rose up while I start makin' breakfast."

"But momma..."

"I said hush now, and see what's keepin' that brother of yours."

"Alright momma," Betty said feeling dismissed, and reluctantly walked out where Fergus was chopping wood.

"Fergus, mom wants you to hurry up with that firewood. She's about to make breakfast." Then Betty asked, "Fergus, are black snakes poisonous?"

Fergus looked up from his chopping.

"Dependin' on what kind of snake. Why?"

"Because a black snake was chasin' me when I went to get the water from the creek this mornin'."

"Really? Is that really true? Come on Betty, I don't believe you," Fergus said.

"Yes, Fergus, it's true, but I could tell momma didn't believe me either."

Just then momma yelled from the doorway, "Fergus, where are

you with that firewood? You're holdin' up breakfast," hoping a little guilt would hurry Fergus along.

"Comin' Ma," Fergus yelled back. Then he turned to Betty and said, "Betty, I'll sure be glad when Howie and Albert can start helpin' out with this choppin'. Com'on, help me with this firewood will ya."

Betty helped carry in the firewood still talking about that black snake.

"Betty, stop talkin' about that snake and help your sisters," Margaret said sternly.

Margaret was the daughter of Irish immigrants from Westmeath County. Margaret was born in Kentucky. However, she sometimes wished she lived in Ireland. Her mom's stories made Ireland seem so beautiful and serene, a far cry from the forest and hills of this small town in Kentucky. She was grateful to have this small farm amongst the hills, but sometimes she got so tired of all the work it took to run the farm along with raising the children. Like most men on farms in the surrounding area, her husband was so busy farming, he didn't have much time for anything else.

She was thinking about all the things that had to be done that day, when she was interrupted by Betty's question.

"Momma, are we all going to the Murphy's shindig tonight?"

"Oh, it is tonight, isn't it? I forgot with all that needs to be done around here. Yes, if you all get your chores done," Margaret responded.

"Betty wants to see that cute boy she met at the general store," Kate piped in.

"Kate, stop it. That's not true," Betty said embarrassed.

"Yes, it is," Kate snapped back.

"Not true," Betty denies the allegation.

"Girls, stop with that kinda talk and eat your breakfast," Margaret said harshly.

"True." Kate couldn't let it go.

"Not." Neither could Betty.

"Girls, what did I say?" This time when Margaret said it, she pounded the table. That got the girls' attention.

"Sorry, ma."

"Sorry, momma."

"Now girls, let's finish our breakfast so we all can get to the chores of the day."

CHAPTER 2

Arvin

Arvin Jamison is the middle child between two sisters, Lily and Elsie. He is big for his age, five feet, 11 inches, slightly built and weighs about 145 pounds. He has dark skin, tanned from the sun, along with his Native American coloring. Elsie is 14, Arvin 17 and Lily is 20 and still lives at home. Usually, by the time a girl reached 16 years of age, she was engaged to be married. Lily, in some families, could be considered an "old maid." Their mother, Arlinda, is a Native American from the Cherokee nation. Arlinda's father, Ovid, stayed in Kentucky to get married instead of walking in the "Trail of Tears."

In 1838 and 1839 as part of President Andrew Jackson's Indian removal policy, the Cherokee nation was forced to give up its land east of the Mississippi River and migrate to an area in Oklahoma. The Cherokee people called this journey the "Trail of Tears" because of its devastating effects. It was estimated that 16, 000 Cherokees were forced from their homes and 4,000 perished on the journey. Many of Ovid's family members, as well as his friends, were among those that died. It was never discussed in their home.

Arvin's father is a preacher man. Arvin has no interest in following his dad in either the ministry or farming. He has city dreams. Their farm took a lot of work and Arvin really didn't take to it too well.

"Thank goodness I don't have to milk those cows." Arvin told Lily and Elsie. "Last time I had to, I fell off the stool and you guys laughed and made fun of me. That was embarrassin'."

"We didn't mean to embarrass you. But, you have to admit you did look funny laying on the ground with the stool on top of you and your hand still holding the cow's teat." Lily answered.

"I know. I felt funny, too. I'll stick to ridin' the hayraker. Although, once, while I was hookin' up those horses to the raker, I did get kicked. My leg was sore for over a week. Just one more reason why farmin' is just not for me." He continued, "I'm done with getting kicked, bit, falling, hauling, raking and weeding. When I get older I'm gonna go to the city and get me a real job."

"You know that Pa wants you to take over the farm when he gets older", Lily reminded him.

"I know, Lily, but I'm gonna go to the city. No matter what."

Arvin and his sisters continued to discuss his city dreams until they were interrupted by their father who was wanting help with the chores. Their farm was considered one of the largest in the county and Arvin's family was considered to be well off, by farmer's standards.

"Arvin, get the sickle mower, we've got work to do."

"Okay, Pa."

Even though Arvin didn't like farming, he loved anything that had moving parts. Machines. Arvin wanted to work with his hands, but not in the dirt. Not on a farm. He liked working on the tractor when his pa would let him. However, working with the sickle mower took a lot of energy and he wanted to save his energy for the dance.

"Pa, can I take the buggy to the dance tonight?"

"What dance?"

"The Murphy's are throwin' a square dance in their barn tonight. Pa, don't ya remember?" Arvin asked.

"Dang, I forgot." His pa replied. "Your mom did mention it to me. Well, Arvin, let's get goin' and get this work done, so you can see that gal you're sweet on," he said teasingly.

"Pa!" Arvin said, slightly embarrassed.

"Well, son, I saw the way you were lookin' at her at the general store."

"Ya, you're right." Arvin admitted. "She is really pretty. Her family has a small farm over the hill. I expect she and her family will be at the Murphy's. At least, I hope so."

Arvin and his pa continued talking while reaping the hay. Arvin was scared to tell his dad about his city dreams, so he just kept that between him and Lily. As soon as they were finished, Arvin sped back to the house to get "slickered up", as he would put it, for the shindig at Murphy's barn.

CHAPTER 3

Shindig at Murphy's Barn

Both families got to Murphy's barn just about the same time. As Fergus and Betty walked in, the fiddlers were playing. Some people were already dancing.

"We're ready to start – grab the lady of your heart. Bow to your partner, bow to your corner and promenade." Called the fiddler.

"Gee Fergus, look at all who showed up." Betty said as they entered the barn. "Gosh, I think every family from miles around are here."

"Well, Betty, it's the first social in months." Fergus replied. "Thank goodness the Murphy's put up this new barn. We haven't had a social in a long time." Fergus continued talking, but lowered his voice to say, "Betty, isn't that the boy you were makin' eyes at?"

"Hush up Fergus." Betty whispered poking him.

"Ouch." Fergus poked her back and said slightly louder, "Look! He's comin' over."

When Betty turned around to see, she came face to face with Arvin.

"Hi Betty, glad you came. Do you remember me? My name is

Arvin. We have a farm in the same county." Arvin continued to ramble nervously until he finally asked, "Would you care to dance?"

"Okay", Betty said. Conscious of his nervousness, she didn't say anymore. She was a bit nervous herself. Arvin took her hand and they joined the circle of dancers.

"Forward and back, do-si-do and circle right or left. Swing your partner on your right...back home...now, swing your partner on your left...back home." Called the fiddler.

Betty and Arvin started feeling more relaxed with each other, and it showed on their smiling faces. They danced every set and were having fun, but both were glad when they heard the announcement.

"Whew, good set all. Fiddlers and I are takin' a rest now. Folks, do the same, set a spell and get some of Anna Belle Murphy's mighty good punch and cookies. We'll be back for another round of dancin' in a spell."

As the fiddlers were leaving the front of the barn Arvin leaned over and asked, "Betty, do you want to get some of that punch?"

"That would be nice." Betty responded and asked, "I was wonderin' how'd you know my name?"

Feeling a little embarrassed he answered, "I saw you at the general store last week and asked the clerk."

"I saw you, too. I wondered who you were, but was too shy to ask the clerk." Betty said.

"I'm glad I wasn't. The clerk also told me that your family has a farm over the hill from ours. Is it a big farm?" Arvin quickly asked.

"No, just chickens, a couple of plow horses and two cows. Big enough I suppose." Betty said and then continued asking, "How about you? Is your farm big?"

"Yes, big enough. Sometimes I feel it is too big. Too much work." Arvin answered and continued letting her in on the secret that he held with Lily. "I really don't like farmin'. My pa wants me to follow in his footsteps. Farmin' just ain't for me. Neither is preachin'."

"Preachin'? Is your dad also a preacher?" Betty asked.

Arvin responded. "Oh, of course you wouldn't know, but my pa is a preacher over in the next county. He preaches on Wednesday nights. Would you like to go with me to hear him sometime? I can pick you up if you ever want to go." Arvin went on to say, "You would really like what he says."

"I'm sure I would." Betty said. "It would be nice to go sometime", then Betty added, "with you."

"Well, then, how about me pickin' you up next week?"

"Oh, I don't know." Betty said. "I'll have to ask Pa. He's kinda strict about me goin' out with boys."

"Betty, we'd be going to church. I'm sure he wouldn't mind you goin' to church, would he?"

"Suppose not. I'll ask him." Betty went on, taking the conversation in another direction and asked, "So, Arvin what do you want to do?"

"What do you mean?" Arvin asked confused by the question.

"Well, you said that you didn't want farmin' or preachin'. Then what do you want to do?" Betty clarified.

"I wanna to go to the city." Arvin responded. "Betty, I have city dreams."

"What are city dreams?" Betty asked. "What does that mean? What city? Arvin, you're not makin' any kind of sense at all."

"Betty, I wanna live with lots of activity. I wanna to live where there are lots of people and big buildin's. I wanna work with or on machines. That would make me happy. Those are my city dreams. I want to go to Chicago." Arvin said excitedly.

"Chicago?" Betty said loudly.

"Yes, Betty, Chicago." Arvin responded just as loud.

"Arvin, that is so far away. How would you get there? When would you go? "What will your pa say? Oh, I'm sorry to ask so many questions, but I never heard anybody talk like this before."

"That's okay, Betty. I understand. I have some of those same questions floating around in my head. I haven't worked everything out yet. I just know I want to go when I get older, and out on my own. Betty, would you ever want to go to a city?" Arvin asked.

"I don't know. Never thought about that. Although, I guess I have dreams, too."

"What are your dreams Betty?"

"I don't really know. I never thought of what I want as dreams. I guess I want to have a house, a home of my own. There are a lot of us in my family and our cabin is pretty small. I would like a place where I could get some privacy. I have to go outside for that now, and it gets mighty cold in the winter to be sittin' outside just to be alone."

"A farm?" Arvin asked quickly.

"Don't know. Don't really know about a farm or not. Just a home of my own."

Betty and Arvin's conversation was interrupted by Betty's father, Bill Malone.

"Betty, we're gettin' ready to leave. Mornin' comes early, ya know." Bill said.

"I know, Pa. Before we leave I want you to meet Arvin Jamison. His family has a farm in our county, on the other side of the hill."

Bill extended his hand out and Arvin met his.

"Nice to meet you Mr. Jamison." Bill said while shaking his hand.

"Nice to meet you Mr. Malone. May I call on your daughter next week?" Arvin asked.

"Well Mr. Jamison, we'll have to see about that." Bill replied with reluctance.

"My dad's a preacher over in the next county in that little white church. I thought Betty might like to go with me next Wednesday evenin'. Would that be okay?" Arvin responded quickly.

"Is your dad here tonight?" asked Bill.

"Yes, Mr. Malone, he's outside." Arvin responded.

"Mr. Jamison-"

"Please call me Arvin." Arvin interrupted.

"Okay, Arvin. I believe we all could use a little preachin'. It wouldn't hurt for all of us to go. I'll stop and talk with your dad on

11

my way to our buggy. We'll bring Betty. Lookin' forward to hearin' your dad."

"Good night Mr. Malone." Arvin replied excitedly.

"Good night Arvin, nice meetin' you. See you next week."

"Good night Betty. It was fun dancin' with you and it was sure nice talkin' to you tonight. Will be lookin' forward to seein' you next week." Arvin said excitedly.

"Yes", Betty replied, "and thank you for sharing your city dreams with me."

CHAPTER 4

Arvin and Betty

The Malone's did go to hear Arvin's pa preach that following week. Wednesday evenings became a routine for the family. Betty and Arvin became inseparable. When they weren't helping on their farms, they spent time with each other.

Betty had fallen in love with Arvin at the dance in Murphy's barn and never stopped thinking of him. She loved all the picnics they went on and the walks they took holding hands. Arvin was very charming and Betty had fallen under his spell right away. She didn't understand how it was that Arvin chose her to be with. He was so handsome and she was so plain. Plain with a freckled face. When Arvin proposed marriage to her, she felt that her dream had come true. She and Arvin would have a home of their own. Betty was happier than she had ever been.

They had a simple wedding at the little white church. Arvin's dad performed the service, gave them a parcel of land to farm, and had a house built for them. The house was small but had a big kitchen and two bedrooms. Betty loved cooking for her and Arvin. She loved their time sitting together in front of the little stone fireplace in the evenings after dinner.

Farming did not last long for Arvin. He convinced Betty to leave their little farm and go to the city. Betty was sad about leaving their home...a home of her own. Of course, she said yes, as all good wives would. Where Arvin was excited about the unknown, Betty was scared of the same unknown. They packed up some of their things, boarded up their small house, and headed off to Chicago.

CHAPTER 5

A New Beginning

"That train ride was our new beginnin', Betty." Arvin said excitedly.

"Not sure about all this, Arvin." Betty replied apprehensively. She went on to say, "There are people everywhere. I've never seen so many people all in one place. So much noise. Buggy's everywhere."

"Yes, Betty, and look at all those machines, modern automobiles. I'm gonna get us one of those someday." Arvin answered with a big smile on his face.

There were trolleys, wagons filled with produce, wagons filled with lumber, people walking every which way, automobiles, horns honking, and in the middle of all this chaos was Arvin and Betty.

"Arvin, nothin' is the same. Smells are different, sounds are so loud, and there's so many buildin's all on top of each other, and they are so big, too." She added, "I bet the food even tastes different here."

"Ya Betty, ain't it excitin'?" Arvin said with his head turning every which way. He wanted to take everything in at once. Arvin already loved the sounds of the city. He even liked the smells. He knew he was standing on the brink of his future. Arvin was feeling free. Free of the farming and free to live his city dreams. He said once again, "Betty, ain't it excitin'?"

Betty wasn't feeling the same way. She was also looking every which way, but not for the same reason. She was hating the sounds and thought the smells were disgusting.

"Oh, I wouldn't call it excitin'. Maybe noisy, smelly, and dirty, but not excitin'. Arvin, where are we gonna stay?"

"Someone told me about settlement houses in the city. Let's find us one." Arvin said excitedly.

"How we gonna do that?" Betty asked with a slight edge of sarcasm. "There's so many buildin's. How are we gonna know which one is this here settlement house that you're talkin' about?"

"There's a group of fellas over there. I'll ask one of them." Arvin answered with confidence.

"Arvin, don't be talkin' to strangers." Betty whispered.

"Betty, it's okay." Arvin said as started to walk away toward the group of fellas that were standing on a corner.

"Be careful Arvin, you don't know them boys."

Arvin waved his hand in a dismissive manner and again started to walk away. He was getting annoyed with Betty's apprehension and didn't understand her concerns. Arvin spotted a bench and suggested that Betty sit down and wait for him. So, Betty sat down and Arvin left her sitting on a bench near the trolley stop. While she was sitting with their bags, Arvin went off to find the location of one of the settlement houses. Betty felt awkward sitting by herself and a bit scared, too. She was relieved when she saw Arvin walking back towards her.

"Those fellas were good guys. Betty, we got us good luck already. There's a couple of these settlement houses not too far from here. Let's go." Arvin said.

Arvin and Betty grabbed their bags and headed down the street in the direction of the settlement houses.

"Arvin, how much further?" Betty asked, feeling exhausted.

"Not sure, but those buildin's ahead sure look big. They must be one of those houses."

They continued to walk another block when Betty asked, "Arvin, do you think this is it?"

"Ya, this is the number those guys gave me. Betty, let's go in."

He took Betty by the arm and guided her through the doorway. They found themselves standing in a large room full of people just milling around. There were couches, chairs and a few tables.

"Arvin, we can't stay here. Everybody is on top of everyone else." Betty said feeling overwhelmed.

Oh, how she wished she was home in her cabin sitting in front of the fireplace with Arvin. She felt grimy after sitting on the train all day and walking around the smelly dirty city. She thought about the creek and how on hot days she would jump in clothes and all. As she looked around the room thoughts of back home filled her head. She felt someone nudge her. It was Arvin.

"Come on Betty, let's find someone that can help us get a room." Arvin said like a child would say "let's go see what Santa left us under the tree."

Settlement houses were important reform institutions in the late nineteenth and early twentieth centuries. Chicago's Hull House was the best-known settlement in the United States, and it was the first. Jane Addams, who was a pioneer American settlement activist, social worker, and philanthropist, co-founded the Hull House with her partner, Ellen Gates Starr. It was also the first settlement house in the United States. These settlements were usually large buildings in crowded immigrant neighborhoods of industrial cities. Soon after Hull House, several more settlement houses popped up throughout Chicago. Some of them included gymnasiums, auditoriums, classrooms, and meeting halls as well as living space and communal dining facilities for residents.

Arvin and Betty happened upon one of the smaller houses. It was close to the garment district, and Arvin was told that the garment factories were hiring people to run the milling machines. The magic word – machines.

"Betty, I talked with the man in charge. He said we could have a private room, if you help out in the kitchen. I told them there ain't nothin' like your fried chicken."

"Arvin, I thought we were both goin' to work so we could get our own place?" Betty objected.

"Ya, but you can still help out in the kitchen, can't you? I really want us to have one of those private rooms."

Betty thought, how could he make that decision for me? Her feeling of being put in a position that she had no say in, just added to her annoyance with this whole city thing.

"Well, I guess I can. But, a lady on the train told me about an agency I can sign up with to do what they call domestic work. You know, watchin' children or cleanin' houses for some of the wealthy folk. So, even though you told the man here that I would work in the kitchen, I'm still gonna find out about this agency."

Arvin dismisses what Betty had said.

"Let's get settled in our room and we can talk about this later. Right now, I want to get cleaned up and meet up with some of the men folk around here."

"I guess I'll go see the kitchen." Betty said frustrated.

Arvin did get cleaned up, and walked outside to look around. He met up with some fellows who were just hanging around smoking and talking. They all said where they were from and it seemed they all shared one thing in common...they all had city dreams.

Betty found her way to the kitchen not knowing who to see or what to expect. She was still feeling somewhat annoyed with Arvin for volunteering her to work in the kitchen. She was greeted by a young girl with long red hair and a friendly smile.

"You are new here, aren't you? What's your name? I'm Mary." Said the young girl with the friendly smile.

"My name is Betty, Betty Jamison." Betty replied.

"Did you just get here?" Mary inquired.

"Yes", said Betty.

"Betty, where did you come from?"

"I'm sorry. I'm nervous about being in the city. My husband and I just got off the train today from Kentucky. I was told I have to help out in the kitchen. Do you know who I talk to?"

"Why, that would be me. I run the kitchen. My parents immigrated from Ireland, and we settled in Ohio. I wanted to come to the city, so I hopped on a train, and here I am. I love the city."

"I'm not so sure about this city. It's my husband's dream to be here. He wants to work with machines."

"Betty, what do you want?" Mary asked.

"I want a home of my own and I had that in Kentucky. We left it for my husband's city dreams. I still want a home of my own."

"Well, Betty, I am sure you will have it again. Come on let me show you around and get you something to eat."

"Thanks Mary, I am a bit hungry. Do you know anything about an agency that I can sign up with to do domestic work?"

"Well, I don't, but there's a lady here that does domestic work. She lives in the communal part of the house." Mary continued, "I think her name is Sally or Sarah. She isn't here now, but I can leave her a note and have her come to your room, is that okay?"

"Yes. Mary, thank you so much for your kindness. I'm havin' a hard time today. I come from a small farm and am not used to all this hustle and bustle."

"You've had a long day. After something to eat and a good night's sleep you'll feel better."

"You're right, Mary. Thanks."

"You're welcome, Betty." Mary said, and showed her to an empty seat at one of the tables. "Now let me get you something to eat."

Mary disappeared through a swinging door and came back with a sandwich and set it down in front of Betty.

"Would you like something to drink?" Mary inquired.

"No, thank you. The sandwich will be just fine. I'll get some water at the drinking fountain over there." Betty replied as she pointed to the corner of the room.

Betty sat quietly eating the sandwich. She was feeling apprehensive and quite alone. She wished she could feel the happiness that Arvin felt, but she didn't. Betty finished her sandwich. As she walked out of the kitchen, she passed Mary and wished her a good night.

Betty found Arvin outside just standing and looking all around. He seemed to be in a trance.

"Betty, isn't it great? Just look at all the people comin' and goin'. So much action. I'm sure gonna like it in this here city."

"Arvin, can we go to our room now? I'm tired and I want to clean up."

"Ya, I suppose. I'm tired, too." Arvin replied.

Their room was down a hall off the communal sitting area. As they passed several people sitting around chatting, Betty was overcome with a wave of nausea. She knew she wasn't physically ill, just overwhelmed with her new surroundings. As Arvin unlocked the door to their room, she started to feel better.

She could see that the room was sparsely furnished. A dark blue overstuffed chair sat in the corner next to a floor lamp that had a small round table attached to its base. A pile of clean linens laid on top of an unmade bed and a dresser with a mirror was against the wall next to the bed. There was a picture of a man and a woman above the bed. The woman was holding a baby. Betty thought there was something sad about the picture. She supposed it was to represent a couple's new beginning. However, she saw sadness in the woman's eyes.

They each set their bags down on the tile floor. After Betty got cleaned up, she walked over to the bed, started unfolding the linens and getting ready to make the bed, when Arvin came over and started helping. Surprised she said, "Thanks Arvin."

As they continued to make the bed, she thought to herself, *Well, maybe the city is good for Arvin after all. He's never helped with bed making before.*

As soon as the bed was made, they plopped down on it. They were both asleep by the time their heads hit the pillows.

CHAPTER 6
Garment Factory

The next morning Betty went to the kitchen to meet Mary, and Arvin excitedly went to one of the factories in the garment district. As he opened the door to the building, he couldn't believe his dream was about to be realized. Machines! He was greeted by a man that escorted him to a seat in a big room where other men were sitting. Arvin was asked his name and told that someone would call him.

Arvin sat with the other men and realized that everyone there was looking for work. He started to get nervous, hoping there were enough jobs for everyone. Then he brought himself back to knowing that luck was with him. He and Betty found their way to the city, met fellas that knew where there was a settlement house, and then they got a private room. He knew he would get a job.

All of a sudden, he heard his name called. "Arvin Jamison."

Arvin jumped up and said, "That's me!"

"Follow me," the man said. "Do you have any experience with machinery?"

"Only with tractors," Arvin quickly replied. "I'm from a farm in Kentucky."

The man never introduced himself and just led Arvin to a room where another man was sitting behind a table.

"This is Smitty," the man said. "He does the hiring for the milling machines." Then he introduced Arvin, "Smitty, this is Arvin Jamison."

Arvin quickly spoke up and said, "Smitty, you are the man I want to talk to. I really want to work with machines."

"Arvin, is it?" Smitty asked.

"Yes sir," Arvin replied.

"Well Arvin, there's not much training and the hours are long. We are short-handed so you will be expected to work 10 hours a day, and sometimes six days a week. The pay is $1.50 a day. If you want the job, you can start tomorrow."

"I sure do! Thanks, I'll be here." Arvin said almost jumping out of his skin with excitement.

Arvin could hardly wait to get back to the settlement house to tell Betty about his new job with the milling machines. This was his dream come true. A new beginning for sure. City dreams. As he was walking back to the settlement house, he heard his name called out. He turned to see where the voice was coming from, and saw a young man waving at him.

"Hey, wait up," the young man called out.

Arvin waited for the young man to catch up and when he did Arvin asked, "Do I know you?"

"No, I saw you on the train and again at the factory this morning. My name is Chester. I heard your name called at the factory. I'm new to the city and don't know anyone here. I come from Lincoln County," Chester said slightly out of breath.

"Nice to meet you, Chester. I'm from Davies County. My wife, Betty, is from Henderson County. We are staying at the settlement house a couple of blocks from here. Where are you staying?"

"Actually, the same place. I'm in the back in what they call the communal living area. I will say, there are a lot of snorers there."

"C'mon, let's walk back together and talk some more. It's good to have a friend here in the city. My wife is workin' in the kitchen.

She can get us something, so we can eat together."

Arvin and Chester continued talking about their farms and families as they walked back to the settlement house. They both talked about their city dreams as well.

"Betty, meet Chester. He's from Lincoln County." Arvin said excitedly as they walked into the kitchen at the settlement house.

"Nice to meet you. Are you new to the city?" Betty asked.

"Ya, came in on the same train as you guys," Chester answered.

Just as Betty was getting ready to say more, Arvin popped up with, "Betty, I got a job workin' with the milling machines at one of the factories in the garment district. I start tomorrow. More good luck for us!"

"Arvin, I'm happy for you," Betty said.

"Chester and me are hungry. Can you get us something to eat?" Arvin asked.

"Yes. I knew you would get a job at one of those garment factories! I made my fried chicken to celebrate. I know my fried chicken is your favorite."

While Betty went off to get two plates for Chester and Arvin, the guys continued talking about their new jobs. It was like listening to two kids in a candy store discussing all the candy. Betty came back with two plates full of her fried chicken and Chester and Arvin gobbled their food down like they had never eaten before. When they were done, Chester thanked Betty and told Arvin he'd see him at the factory the next day. Arvin asked Betty for another helping of her fried chicken after Chester left. Betty brought Arvin more chicken and a plate full for herself, as well.

As Betty sat down to eat, Arvin asked, "Did you find out anything about that agency you've been talking about?"

"No, Arvin, I didn't. I had to work in the kitchen today and prepare food for tonight's dinner," Betty answered.

"Oh, that's nice. Isn't it exciting? I'm gonna be workin' with machines! It'll be hard work, but I am willin' to work hard just to have a chance to be with all those machines. I'll be workin' with the material that's gonna be making men's suits. Someday, I'm gonna get me one of those fancy suits. Since I start the job tomorrow morning, you need to make me breakfast early. Will that be a problem?" Arvin asked.

"No, Arvin, that won't be a problem since I'm workin' the kitchen in the mornin'." Betty answered.

Arvin, still enjoying Betty's fried chicken, continued to talk about his new job and barely listening to what Betty had to say. He was all into his city dreams and couldn't wait to get to those machines. They barely spoke on the way to their room. Betty went to bed exhausted. She had worked in the kitchen all day preparing her famous chicken for supper. Since Mary wasn't feeling well, she had to prepare lunch for the house, as well. She was asleep before her head hit the pillow. Arvin followed suit.

Arvin and Betty were both up before dawn. Arvin was anxious to get to work and Betty needed to open the kitchen. Arvin got his breakfast and was so excited about his new job that he barely tasted what he was eating.

As he got up to leave, Betty said, "Bye Arvin. I'm gonna find out about that agency this afternoon. I packed you some fried chicken. See you tonight. I love you."

"Bye Betty." Arvin shouted back. "See you tonight."

CHAPTER 7

Serena

With tears in her eyes, Betty went back to their room to get cleaned up and changed for the day. She was feeling a little left out of Arvin's life. He hadn't listened to her at supper and it was obvious he had not been interested in what she had to say. Now this morning he didn't say "I love you" when he left for his job. Betty thought it best just to excuse his behavior and chalk it up to his excitement about their new life in the city. However, Betty still didn't feel better. She was lost in her thoughts and trying to let her sadness go when she heard a knock at the door. Betty answered the door and a saw young lady with long beautiful dark hair with green eyes that looked like marbles.

"Are you Betty?" The young lady asked.

"Yes," Betty answered.

"Mary told me that you wanted some information about a domestic agency."

"You must be Sally or Sarah." Betty said.

"You got the S right, my name is actually Serena." The young lady replied.

"Nice to meet you Serena. I want to do some domestic work. Some lady that I met on the train told me about an agency."

"The agency I work with is just a couple blocks away. Come on, Betty, I'll take you."

"Let me just grab my wrap and we can go. My husband started at one of the garment factories today. So, he won't be back until tonight."

"Good, we can stop for some coffee and pastry."

"That would be nice, but I don't have enough money," Betty said, embarrassed.

"Betty, today will be my treat. Let's go."

Serena guided Betty down the walkway to catch the streetcar. Betty's head was turning every which way. She started to feel overwhelmed again with all the noise of people driving wagons, people walking here and there, dodging automobiles and all the different sounding horns.

Betty cleared her head and focused on getting to the agency with Serena. Just as she was getting used to being on a moving train within the city, she could feel Serena nudging her towards the steps of the streetcar indicating that this is where they were to get off. She started to get butterflies in her stomach. A combination of nerves and excitement came over her. This is for real. She is in the city living Arvin's city dreams...but were they hers? She didn't have time to answer herself as Serena guided her down the street into the doorway of the agency. Serena approached a lady that was sitting behind a desk.

"Good morning Marie, this is Betty Jamison. Betty and her husband just arrived from Kentucky and she's looking for domestic work. Can you help her?" Serena asked.

"Good morning Serena," Marie replied. She turned to Betty with a reassuring smile and asked, "Betty Jamison, is it?"

"Yes. Arvin, my husband, and me are stayin' at the settlement house a ways from here and I want to sign up so I can get some work," Betty replied.

"Betty, how old are you?" asked Marie.

"Eighteen," Betty answered shyly.

"Have you done any sitting on children?" Marie inquired.

"I took care of my younger brothers and sisters, does that

count?"

"That depends. Do you cook?"

"Yes, I'm a fair cook. My specialty is fried chicken."

"We could give you a try. I have a family that has four-year old twins, a boy and a girl. The mother died of pneumonia. The father is a doctor at Mercy Hospital on 26th Street. You'd have to take a streetcar to his house on Jackson Boulevard. He will pay you a dollar a day, plus your streetcar fare. Your duties would include cooking. I can send you there tomorrow to meet Dr. Russell for his approval of you."

"Oh, goodness. I don't know what to say. What time will I have to go tomorrow?" Betty asked.

"Don't worry, I'll give you all the information before you leave. In the meantime, can you write?"

"Yes...a little," Betty replied, slightly embarrassed.

"Then, please fill in your name and the address of the settlement house."

Marie handed Betty a pen and some paper.

"But I only know the name of the street, is that okay?" Betty asked.

"Yes," Marie said.

Serena helped Betty answer the questions and fill out the paperwork. Betty finished and as she was handing the paperwork back to Marie she asked, "How's, that? Did I do fine?"

"Yes, you did. Here's the address and directions plus streetcar fare. Dr. Russell is going to like you, I know it," Marie answered.

"Marie, I can take Betty to the streetcar. It's the same one I take to Mrs. White's." Serena said.

"Thanks Serena." Marie replied and then said to Betty, "Welcome to our city."

Betty smiled and said good-bye. She really didn't understand why everyone she had met so far really liked this city. She much preferred the serenity of the hills and forests of home.

Serena interrupted her thoughts with, "Betty, it looks like you're buying pastry next time."

"Hush, Serena. I don't have the job yet."

"You'll get it, as pretty as you are, and I tasted your fried chicken. Maybe you should bring Dr. Russell some." Serena said with a chuckle.

They both laughed. Betty was feeling more relaxed now. She was also feeling so grateful for finding a friend like Serena. They were still laughing as they entered the pastry shop.

"I'm gonna have me one of those doughnuts," Serena told the clerk behind the counter.

"I'll take one of those, too," Betty chimed in.

"Two doughnuts and two coffees," repeated the clerk.

"Thanks Serena for being so kind to me. You and Mary have sure made me feel at home. I wasn't sure I would like it here, I'm still not. Arvin is so sure of himself and is all excited about bein' in this big city and his job workin' with machines." Betty said, then asked, "What do I do about the kitchen now that I might be workin'?"

"Betty, you will be working. Not might. You now have two friends and once you start working, things will look better to you. Talk to Mary about working in the kitchen. She's really understanding and will work with you." Serena suggested.

The two of them sat, drinking coffee and talking for an hour or so. Betty told her about how she grew up on a farm, how she met Arvin and when they got married. Serena shared more about her family in Ohio. Her dad, older brothers and uncles all worked in the steel mills. Most of Ohio's industry came from the steel mills. She moved to Chicago to be part of something new and different. She found Chicago to be exciting. Betty just shook her head. They finished and set off to get back to the settlement house.

That night, Betty tried to talk to Arvin about her day at the agency and the pastry shop. Arvin was just too busy talking to the fellas outside about his job. He wasn't interested in woman's business. When he finally came in to get one of the cookies that Betty had made, he asked her if she got a job. All she said was "yes" and then went to their room for the night. Betty was tired and annoyed. She felt it best to go right to bed before she said something to Arvin she would regret.

CHAPTER 8

Dr. Russell

The early morning sounds of the city woke Betty. She looked around and saw Arvin was already gone. She wondered why he didn't wake her up to get his breakfast. Pulling out one of better cotton dresses, she washed up, and put it on. When she got to the kitchen to check in with Mary she found out that Arvin had stopped in for some of the biscuits she made the night before. Betty grabbed some herself and met Serena.

"Serena, thanks for taking me to the streetcar. There's no streetcars where I come from. I'm nervous," Betty said.

"You'll be fine. Anyone who can take a train to an unknown place is brave," Serena replied reassuring Betty.

"Thanks for the encouragement. I don't feel very brave," Betty said apprehensively.

"Betty, this is my stop. This is where I get off. Now remember, you get off the next time the streetcar stops." Serena said as she stepped off the streetcar. She shouted back, "Good luck."

"Thanks!" Betty said loudly.

Betty sat on the edge of her seat waiting for the trolley to stop. She was worried she would miss it or not get up in time to get off. When it did, Betty sprung up from her seat just like one of those toys when wound up a clown pops out on a spring. She grabbed a hold of the pole by the door and carefully stepped down onto the two steps and off in to the street.

Betty's mind started to have all kinds of racing questioning thoughts. *Oh dear. So many people walkin' every which way. I got off alright. Now to find the right number house. I don't know if I can do this. These houses are big, bigger than the ones by the settlement house. What did Marie say? The house was yellow and grey and the number was 45. I sure hope I'm goin' the right way. So much noise. I've been walkin' a while now. Oh, where is that house? There. No, it's yellow alright, no grey. I am gettin' scared. There's another yellow house, oh please let that be the house. Forty-five...this is it!*

Betty nervously walked up the two steps and knocked on door. She was shaking inside and wasn't sure if her knees were knocking together or if it was the wind blowing the bottom of her skirt. The door opened and a man in his late 20's opened the door.

"Dr. Russell?" Betty quickly asked.

"You must be the lady that the agency sent over. Come in," Dr. Russell said.

"Thank you," Betty politely responded.

Dr. Russell invited Betty to sit down on the sofa and began their conversation.

"Your name is Mrs. Jamison, Betty Jamison, is that right?"

"Yes," Betty replied.

"How old are you Mrs. Jamison?"

"Eighteen, I'll be Nineteen in a couple of months."

"Marie told me you helped your mom with your siblings and that you can also cook, is that right?"

"Yes, I took care of my little brothers and sisters, and I'm a fair cook. Fried chicken is my favorite thing to fix."

"That sounds good, I can't wait to try some. Cora, Tommy, come meet Mrs. Jamison." Dr. Russell responded with a smile on his face.

"Are you gonna be our new mother?" Cora asked.

"No. Mrs. Jamison is going to watch you while I am at the

hospital...and she fixes fried chicken, your favorite," Dr. Russell quickly responded.

"Yay!" Both twins squealed in unison.

"Do you want to play?" Tommy asked excitedly.

"Dr. Russell, do you want me to stay today?" Betty asked.

"Yes, I think you are perfect for our family. I am not working today. So, I'll show you where everything is and you can get to know Cora and Tommy. I work at Mercy hospital, which is on the outskirts of the city. Did Marie tell you that you would be working five days a week and weekends sometimes fall within those five days? My work shift changes each week."

"She probably did. I was so excited about getting a job, that I didn't hear every word she said, but the schedule is just fine."

"Mrs. Jamison, I hope you still feel that way after spending a week with the twins."

Betty did stay the day and got the lay of the land. Playing with Cora and Tommy was a delight. They were both very well-mannered and behaved. She did make her fried chicken and they all voted it was the best fried chicken they ever had. Fried chicken was added to the weekly menu of dinners. At the end of the day, Dr. Russell and the twins walked Betty to the streetcar and said goodbye. As Betty climbed the stairs of the trolley, she turned around and waved feeling a little better about being in the city.

On the ride back to the settlement house, she replayed the day in her mind. She was thinking how so much had changed for her in the last couple of days. Betty was trying to sort out her feelings when she realized the trolley was coming to her stop. She stepped down onto the street and walked back to the settlement house with a little bounce in her step. Yep, she was feeling better about being in the city. She couldn't wait to tell Arvin.

Betty saw Arvin standing outside the settlement house just looking around. Excitedly, Betty approached him and said, "Arvin, I can't wait to tell you about my day."

Arvin not really listening to what Betty said replied, "Isn't the city exciting? Learning the machines is also exciting. Even though we've only been here for a couple of days, I've feel like I have always been here. Met some guys who are from Indiana and Ohio. I guess we all had the same city dreams. Let's get some of that great food you prepared in the kitchen."

Betty tried again to get Arvin's attention. "Arvin, I want to tell you all about Dr. Russell and the twins."

"Later, Betty, I'm hungry and tired," Arvin replied.

With that Arvin went into the settlement house and walked toward the kitchen with Betty trailing him. Upon entering the kitchen, he grabbed a tray, some food, found an empty table, and plopped down on one of the chairs. Betty joined him and they both ate in silence.

Just as Betty was finishing up her supper, Serena came over to their table. Arvin excused himself and went outside to talk to some fellas he knew from the factory.

"Betty, how'd your day go?" Serena asked.

"Dr. Russell is so nice and the twins are really well behaved. I can't thank you enough for takin' me to that agency. How was your day?" Betty asked.

"Same. I clean for a family, Mr. and Mrs. White, and do their cooking as well. They have a nanny for their three kids. One of the kids is touched in the head. That nanny has her hands full. So glad I only have to cook and clean. Enough about me. What did Arvin say about your new job?" Serena inquired.

"He was too busy tellin' me about his and about how hungry and tired he was. We used to spend time together and even did some of our farm chores together. The last two days I feel like I'm with a stranger."

"Things will get better. Things are all new to both of you. It took me a couple of weeks to get settled in. It seems you've' gotten settled into the kitchen alright, everybody really liked those apple pies you made. Betty, when did you have time to make them?"

"I made them early this mornin'. I saw the apples last night and remembered my momma's pies. I miss my home Serena. Arvin's parents gave us a parcel of land to live on and farm. After a year, Arvin just couldn't do it anymore. He said he had to go to the city. I knew that he had city dreams before I married him. So, I didn't complain and helped close up our land and here we are."

"Like I said, things will get better. It's getting late. I best get to bed. You should go, too." Serena said.

"You're right. See you in the morning." Betty replied.

"Good night Betty." Serena said as she walked toward the hall on her way to retire.

Betty bid Serena good night and once again felt left out. She thought even though Arvin was never much of a talker, at least he had shown interest in what she did. Now it seems he is only interested in what he does and wants to just talk about that to anyone who will listen. Betty went to their room. Arvin was still outside talking with the fellas from the factory. She fell asleep the minute her head hit the pillow. She never heard Arvin come in and climb into bed, nor feel his kiss goodnight.

CHAPTER 9
Teddy Roosevelt

Serena had been right, things did get better for Betty and Arvin. Arvin loved his job at the garment factory and had made some close friends over the past two years. Betty was getting on nicely with Dr. Russell, Cora, and Tommy. Her relationship deepened with Serena. Her fried chicken had become famous at the settlement house, along with her pies. Arvin got better at listening to Betty and they both decided they wanted to get a place of their own as soon as they could.

One afternoon Dr. Russell said to Betty, "Mrs. Jamison, I need you to stay a little longer tomorrow. I am on a team of doctors that will be treating our former President, Teddy Roosevelt. Since it may be late, I can take you back to the settlement house. Will this be okay with your husband?"

"Yes, I'll tell him tonight. He's been workin' late these nights. So, I don't think it will make no never mind to him. What happened to Mr. Roosevelt?" Betty asked.

"He decided to run again for the white house and was giving a campaign speech in Milwaukee, Wisconsin, about 100 miles from here. From what I understand, he was shot in the chest. However, the local hospital took x-rays and they saw that the bullet was lodged against his fourth rib. So, it never reached his heart. I guess the bullet got stopped by his thick overcoat, his eyeglass case and 50 pages of paper that was to be his speech. He is coming into Mercy and will be staying awhile recuperating."

"Why, Dr. Russell, you'll be famous!" Betty exclaimed.

"No, I don't think so. My team and I are just watching over him. He is no longer in danger. Just a rest, that's all."

Theodore Roosevelt, Jr., was an author, statesman, soldier, naturalist and reformer who served as the 26th President of the United States from 1901 to 1909. As a leader of the Republican Party during this time, he became a driving force for the Progressive Era in the early 20th century

CHAPTER 10

Two Years Later

Over the next two years Arvin and Betty worked hard and saved enough money to start looking for their own place. Then something happened to cause them to speed up the plan.

"Arvin, what are we gonna do now that we're gonna have a baby?" Betty asked.

"These last two years have been hard on us Betty. But, with you puttin' in all those hours with those kids and me workin' at the factory extra hours, we have enough money to get us a place in one of those courtyard buildings," Arvin replied.

"Really?" Betty asked, looking surprised.

"Yes, really. I'll start askin' around about those kinds of buildings tomorrow."

"I can ask Mary. She's been overseein' the kitchen for several years and has seen a lot of people comin' and goin' from this here settlement house," Betty quickly replied.

"Betty, this is man's doin'. Leave the findin' out to me," Arvin said firmly.

A little hurt, Betty asked, "But Arvin, can it hurt, me askin'?"

"Okay, but wait until I can do some checkin' around first." Arvin answered reluctantly.

"Alright," Betty said acquiescing.

Arvin's buddies from the factory did help him find a place in one of the courtyard buildings. It was on the near north side of Chicago. It was perfect, and he knew Betty would be excited. So, he made the deal, and it was a good deal. Arvin negotiated the price down for the rent and was able to get the manager to let them move in right away. He couldn't wait to tell Betty and show her how man's business is done. Arvin felt like a big man and crowed to anyone who would listen about his first "business deal." There would be many more to come.

Betty was excited, especially about the part of moving in right away. It did take several trips on the trolley, however, they finally got settled in. She couldn't wait to tell Dr. Russell and her family about their new place.

As soon as Betty got the twins settled, she started telling Dr. Russell about her new home.

"Dr. Russell, me and Arvin did get a place of our own and we already moved in. It's in one of those courtyard buildin's. There's three rooms. The kitchen has a stove and an ice box. My momma would've loved to have had an icebox and have a man actually deliver a block of ice for the box. I never saw such a thing. He puts the ice block through a little door on the outside porch and it goes right into the ice box. It'll be nice to be cookin' in my own kitchen for just me and Arvin and not for all the people at the settlement house. The bedroom has a pull down bed and a small alcove, where our baby can sleep. There's also a big front room with bay windows. You can see the street from that room. We have a place in the front of the buildin'. It's real nice. Here I am goin' on and on." Betty said, and added, "I'm just so happy."

"I'm so happy for you Betty. How were you able to move in already? It's only been two days since you've been here," Dr. Russell replied.

"Arvin made a deal with the manager. He and his buddies found it in the morning and we started moving in that afternoon. It took a lot of trips on the trolley, but it was worth it," Betty answered.

"Let me know if you need anything. You've been so good for the twins."

"Thanks Dr. Russell. Some of the people from the settlement house gave us some pots, pans, and some dishes, too. They was extra from the kitchen I was helpin' out in. If you have any old sheets or towels, could use some of them."

"I'll see what I can do Betty. Now, I must be on my way to the hospital. See you tonight, and congratulations on getting your own place."

CHAPTER 11

The Hoosier Cabinet

Betty and Arvin enjoyed their new home the next month with little or no furniture. Betty didn't care. She loved cooking in her kitchen and found some crates that she and Arvin could eat on. Life continued for Arvin and Betty without incidents beside the normal grind at the factory for Arvin and the twins for Betty. Then one afternoon good luck came to them, as Arvin would say. Arvin gathered up some of his buddies from the factory and arranged for all of them to help surprise Betty. Once again, his wheeling and dealing paid off.

Arvin and his buddies finished putting everything in place before Betty got home. She didn't know that Arvin had talked someone from the factory into giving them a crib and dressing table for the soon to arrive baby. Some folks at the settlement house had chipped in and bought them a kitchen table and four wooden chairs, and Arvin had bought a sofa and a couple of side tables, along with lamps for each table from a furniture repossession store. However, the biggest surprise to Betty was going to be a Hoosier cabinet for the kitchen. They all sat back and admired their work. They were pretty proud of themselves.

Arvin's buddies left and Arvin sat down on the sofa and just watched the traffic through their big picture window. He was thinking how he had done it again. How he did strike up some great deals...when he heard the doorknob rattle.

Arvin called out, "Betty, is that you?"

"Yes, Arvin, it's me. I don't know how to get this key to work. Let me in," Betty called back.

Arvin opened the door and said, "Here, let me show you, just turn the key this way. It's a little hard, needs oil. I'll see to it tomorrow. Come in. I have a surprise for you."

The first thing Betty saw was the Hoosier cabinet.

"Oh goodness, look at that. How did you get that? That must of cost us all of the money we had," Betty said with surprise.

"I bought it from a fella at work. He and his wife were movin' in with his folks and didn't have the room for it. I got it cheap. Do you like it?"

"Arvin, I love it. Look, it has a pull out, tilt down, flour bin and one for sugar, too. So many drawers. I can't wait to start rollin' out my pie dough on this counter. So much room."

Then she saw the table and chairs.

"Where did these pretty wooden chairs come from?" Betty asked.

"Some of the people from the settlement house chipped in and bought this table and chairs for us. They brought them over this afternoon. Go look in the front room," Arvin suggested.

Betty had tears in her eyes as she walked into the other room.

"A sofa and tables and lamps. I've dreamed about havin' pretty furniture like this," Betty said with tears in her eyes.

"I made a great deal with a store that repossesses furniture from people who couldn't make the arranged payments. I used some of our savin's but since I made such a great deal I couldn't pass it up. It'll be nice to sit in this room by the window and watch all the cars and action outside."

"You are becoming a master wheeler and dealer. Oh Arvin, it'll be nice to just to sit on something soft. Those hard chairs at the settlement house were so uncomfortable and were hard to sit in, so straight up and down."

"One last thing, then let's eat 'cause I'm gettin' hungry. Go into our bedroom."

"There's more?" Betty asked in a high voice.

"Ya Betty, there's more. Come on and see."

Betty walked into the bedroom and when she saw the alcove she said with tears in her eyes, "A crib? And a dressin' table? Where? How?"

"I got both from someone at the factory. His baby is too big for them and they're not plannin' on havin' any more kids, since they have three already. I talked them into just giving them to me. They do need a good scrubbin' tho."

By this time Betty was actually crying with joy and disbelief.

"I can make them look brand new. Thank you Arvin for gettin' all this stuff. I can't believe all this. I'm so happy. It's like a dream," Betty said through her tears.

"Betty, can we eat now?"

"Of course! You deserve a good meal for all the work you've done here. Let's go sit on our new chairs and eat off our new table"

"Ya, after carryin' all this stuff, I worked up a big appetite. Right now, I'm so hungry I could eat a cow. I'm pretty tired too. Factory got in a big order so all of us workers have to go in extra early tomorrow."

"I made a chicken casserole for Dr. Russell, and extra for us. Let me just get it out of my bag."

"Betty, if nothin' else, you're a good cook," Arvin declared.

"Thanks Arvin and there's even enough for seconds," Betty answered.

Arvin and Betty continued to talk over supper. Actually, Betty just listened to Arvin boast about what a wheeler dealer he was.

All of a sudden he stopped boasting and said, "I think I'll just help myself to some more of this here casserole. Mighty good."

"Thanks again, Arvin. Dr. Russell may get us some sheets and towels, isn't that nice?" Betty replied.

"Yeah, but we don't need no handouts. You're gettin' might chummy with that Dr. Russell, aren't you?" Arvin said sarcastically.

"Stop, you're being silly. He's just grateful because I take such good care of his twins. Plus, he's a nice, honorable man."

"Ya, sure," Arvin said again sarcastically.

Betty ignored his remark and just continued on with her conversation while they went into the front room to enjoy their new sofa.

"I'm gonna have Serena come over next week for tea. She hasn't seen our new place and I want to use some of our nice cups and saucers that your folks gave us for our wedding. I think I'll make some nice bread to go with our tea. Wait until she sees this Hoosier cabinet and the rest of the stuff. She is gonna be so happy for us. I'm so glad that nonsense of those women marching is over. She wouldn't have been able to get thru all those women with signs. What were those signs all about anyway? Arvin? Arvin?" Betty looked at Arvin slumped over with his head on the arm of their new sofa fast asleep, knowing he hadn't heard a word she said.

Chicago was home to one of the nation's most robust women's suffrage movements. Women were marching in Chicago for women's right to vote. Women could be seen carrying signs on the busiest streets in the city. The suffragettes' effort led to a big victory in 1913 when Illinois women won the right to vote in presidential and local races. Illinois became the first state east of the Mississippi River that allowed women to vote in the presidential election.

CHAPTER 12

Girl Talk

Betty was just cleaning up her Hoosier cabinet when she heard a knock at the door. She was so excited, for she knew it had to be Serena. She put her rag down and ran to the door to open it.

"Oh, Serena, I'm so happy to see you," Betty said as she was opening the door. "Come in."

"Betty, I'm so happy to see you as well. I've missed you so much, and of course, everyone at the settlement house misses your delicious southern fried chicken," Serena said.

"Although I miss some of the people at the settlement house, can't say I miss the house very much."

"Yes, I agree." As Serena looked around the apartment she exclaimed, "You have a real nice place here, so warm and homey. Oh, and you have a Hoosier cabinet. How wonderful. Mrs. White has one and it's so nice to prepare meals on the counter. You are going to love it."

"I know. I've already used it to make bread for us today. Come look at what someone from Arvin's work gave us. A crib and a dressin' table. I need to clean them both up, but when I do, they will look brand new."

"That was so nice. I'm so happy for you and I see that you got the table and chairs from the people at the settlement house."

"Yes, and I love them."

"I'm glad you guys got out of the settlement house, especially since your baby will be born soon. Do you have a midwife?"

"Yes, there is a lady in this buildin' that's a midwife. Arvin says, "Luck continues to be with us."

"Betty, although Arvin may be right, both of you have worked really hard over the last four years. Quite frankly, I don't know how you kept up working in the kitchen and for Dr. Russell. You are a strong woman, Betty, stronger than most."

"Sometimes I don't feel very strong. I just do what needs to be done. Arvin is so busy at the factory and with some of the guys there that he's not around much. Dr. Russell has been so kind to me, to us, that working for him has not been all that hard."

"Are you going to work for him until the baby is born?"

"No, I'm workin' for one more week. The baby is due in three weeks."

"What's Dr. Russell going to do?"

"He hired someone thru the agency to be with the twins after school and to cook and clean for him temporarily. Dr. Russell wants me to come back and bring the baby with me after a month. He says that I'm like family to him and the twins. He's changin' his work schedule at the hospital to three days a week, so I'll only be workin' those three days. Arvin and I will miss some of the money, but Arvin got himself a raise so we'll be okay. Plus, I'm gonna take in ironin'. I can do that at home and be with the baby. Maybe Arvin's right, luck continues to be with us. Well, enough about me and Arvin. Let's have some tea. Like I said, I have some special homemade bread for us".

"I think that Dr. Russell is sweet on you," Serena said.

"Hush up now and try some of my homemade bread," Betty said looking a little flushed.

"Okay, but I still say-"

Betty quickly interrupted with, "Now, stop with that nonsense. Let me pour you some tea."

Serena and Betty chatted over tea all afternoon. Betty felt alive with joy seeing her friend after so long. Serena was really her only close friend. They talked about recipes, baby names, Dr. Russell, and the latest fashions. Serena was still working for the White family. One of their children was just sent to Dunning, a medical and psychiatric facility or to some known as an insane asylum. She said Mrs. White hasn't been the same since. Serena feared she may lose her job due to the husband threatening to take the other two children and leaving. The afternoon flew by. When Serena got up to leave, they promised each other they would see each often. Betty walked Serena to the door and waved to her as she walked down the stairs.

Betty poured herself another cup of tea. She walked into the front room and looking out of the front window, she could see Serena waiting for the streetcar. All of a sudden, she felt homesick.

Arvin got home just as Serena was leaving. Betty made a quick supper, they ate, and then had their coffee in their front room. Sitting on their new couch, Betty and Arvin watched the activity through their big picture window, until it was time to retire for the night. Their sleep was short lived.

CHAPTER 13

Just Breathe

"Arvin, it's time," Betty said excitedly while poking at Arvin.

"Time for what?" Arvin asked sleepily.

"Arvin!" Betty yelled.

"Betty, it's in the middle of the night.....oh, you mean, the baby?" Arvin said as he jumped out of bed.

"Yes, go get the midwife. We're gonna have us a baby," Betty declared.

Arvin ran up the stairs in his sleepy stupor, knocked on several wrong doors before finding the right one, and the midwife. When the door opened, he said, in much too loud of a voice for the middle of the night, "My wife is having a baby. Please come downstairs and help her, help us."

The face behind the door said, "Let me get my wrap and my bag." The door closed and the face reappeared and said, "Ready to go."

On the way down the stairs she asked, "What's your wife's name?"

"Betty." Arvin answered.

As they entered the apartment. Betty saw them and was relieved and happy to see Arvin with the midwife.

47

"Betty, how you doing?" The midwife asked.

"Doin' just fine. As long as I keep grittn' my teeth and clenchin' my fists," Betty answered.

"Arvin, you know what to do now. Get us water and some clean rags," instructed the midwife.

"What's your name?" Betty asked.

"Helen," replied the midwife.

"Thanks Helen for comin'. I knew you were in the buildin', just never got to meet you," Betty said.

"That's okay, Betty, we're meeting now. We're going to do this together. Can you lay back and put your legs up bending them at the knees?"

"Yes."

"How's the pain?"

"Not so good. Hurts like a son of a gun," Betty said while breathing hard.

"Are the pains coming and going?"

"Yes. Every couple of minutes or so," Betty managed to say in between the pains.

"Okay, I 'm going to check to see how things are coming. Just push your knees apart so I can check you. That's right. Just keep breathing. No, don't hold your breath. I know it hurts, but just keep breathing in and out. Things look good. The head is in position, but not quite ready to come out yet. When the pains start coming really fast that means the baby is getting ready... and when that time comes, you will need to push. Like I said, we will do this together. I will help you."

After a few minutes, Betty asked, "Helen, how are things?"

"Going just the way things should go." Helen answered.

Just then Arvin popped into the bedroom and said, "Helen, I got to get me to work. Will you stay with Betty?"

"Of course. I will stay with her for as long as she needs me. Now, go on and get to work. You are going to need that pay, for you'll be having another mouth to feed soon," Helen replied.

Arvin smiled and said, "Betty, I'll see you tonight. Helen will stay and take care of you."

"Bye Arvin," Betty said and waved goodbye.

Just after Arvin left Betty's contractions started coming faster.

"Helen, pains, lots of them. Ow, ow, OW!" Betty said while trying to hold her breath.

"Breath Betty, I see the baby's head. Now when I say push, push. It's going to hurt, but don't stop. The baby is just about ready."

Betty let out a loud, "E-ow!"

"Good, that last pain did it. The baby dropped, now push," Helen said encouragingly.

Betty pushed as had as she could.

"Good Betty. Now, let's change positions. Let me help you roll on your side." Betty rolled to her side once again holding her breath. Helen saw that and said, "Don't hold your breath. Breathe Betty."

Betty listened and started to take short breaths.

"Now Betty, let me roll you back. When we get you on your back, put your hand under your bust on your abdomen and when you feel the tightening, push by breathing into the pain."

Betty did as Helen instructed her. Helen continued with her instruction and said, "Now, push one more time."

Betty pushed and let out one more loud, "Eeee-ow!"

"That did it!" Helen exclaimed. "Beautiful baby girl. Listen to that cry. When I slapped her bottom, I felt the sting on my hand and that is good luck, so I've been told." Helen said and then asked, "Betty, how you doing? You okay?"

"Doin' okay, I guess. Is the baby okay?" Betty asked.

"Well, see for yourself," Helen said, holding the baby up for Betty to see. "Here is your beautiful baby girl." Then Helen laid the baby by Betty.

"Look at all that hair. Why, she needs a hair trim already," Betty said in a tired voice.

"You haven't lost your sense of humor, that's good. Betty, you are a very strong woman. Most women I help cry and scream and won't do as I ask. You were wonderful. Yes, very strong. Do you have a name for her?"

"Ruth. I thought we'd call her Ruth. She is a pretty thing, isn't she?"

"Yes, she is, and Ruth is a real nice name." Helen answered.

Arvin and Betty didn't get much sleep the next month. Ruth was displaying a mind of her own and Arvin would say "she's a chip off the old block." Betty hated that saying.

Since it was early, she decided to make some fresh bread while Ruth was sleeping. She was just punching the dough when there was a knock at the door. Betty wiped her hands and went to the door. As she opened it, she got quite a surprise.

"Why Dr. Russell, what are you doin' here? Please, come in," Betty said.

Dr. Russell stepped inside and said, "Came to see your new baby and to bring you sheets and towels."

"That's so nice. Thank you."

"What did you have?"

"A baby girl. I'll go see if she's sleepin'," she said as she walked toward the bedroom. Ruth was stirring so, Betty picked her up and brought her out to meet Dr. Russell. "This is Ruth. Ruth, meet Dr. Russell."

"Betty, she is beautiful and looks good. Have you taken her to a doctor yet?"

"Yes, I took her to the clinic down the street. They gave her a shot."

"That was the pertussis vaccine, to prevent whooping cough."

"Yes, that's what they said," Betty went back to the bedroom and laid Ruth back in her crib. When she walked back into the kitchen, she asked, "Dr. Russell, would you like a cup of coffee?"

"No thank you. Betty, I've been thinking and I don't want you and Ruth on the streetcar in the morning. Too many people. Too much of a chance that your baby could get sick. Now that you live closer, I can pick you up and take you home. I'll pick you up after the twins leave for school."

"Dr. Russell, that's so nice."

"Betty, you're family to us, and now Ruth is part of our family. I will pick you up this coming Tuesday."

"I'll be ready. Thanks for comin' by and thanks again for the sheets and towels."

"You are quite welcome Betty." Dr. Russell responded. Betty walked him to the door and bid him goodbye.

CHAPTER 14
Betty's Juice Joint

Dr. Russell left and Betty started preparing something for dinner. Ruth was still sleeping, so she finished setting the table. Betty was just pulling the bread out of the oven when Arvin got home.

She greeted him and said, "Arvin, Ruth is sleeping, and dinner is ready. So, if you want a quiet meal, clean up and come to the table."

"Just give me a couple of minutes, it's been a hard day. Workin' at the factory really isn't turnin' out like I thought my "city dream" would. I talked to a couple of guys and we may want to be startin' somethin' on our own."

"What?" Betty asked with a questioning look.

"Well, don't really know. Just heard these guys talkin' about stuff."

"What stuff?"

"Don't know yet. I'll be talkin' to them guys again." Arvin answered somewhat annoyed by being questioned.

"Well, be careful Arvin, don't get yourself into somethin' that could cause you or us trouble."

Even more annoyed now by Betty's response, he said with a

slight sarcastic tone, "Betty, you worry too much. You just take care of woman's business and let me take care of man's business."

Betty responded with a sarcastic tone of her own, "If you say so, Arvin." Then she continued with a softer tone, "Dr. Russell came by today. I go back to work for him on Tuesday. I'll only be workin' three days a week."

"What? Why?" Arvin asked, somewhat surprised.

"His schedule at the hospital changed. He came by to bring us some towels and sheets."

"Why would he do that?"

"He had asked me what we needed for our new place, so I told him sheets and towels."

"I don't know, Betty, you're getting mighty personal with him. I don't like it. You're his worker, his, what do you call it, his domestic help," Arvin said with that tone again.

"Dr. Russell considers me part of his family. After all, I've been with those twins for over four years now. Since we moved closer to his place, he's gonna pick Ruth and me up so we don't have to take the streetcar."

"Hmm, I think he looks at you different than family."

"Arvin, stop. Since when are you so jealous?"

"Not jealous, just worried," Arvin snapped back quickly.

"Like you said, you take care of man's business and I'll take care of woman's business...and this is woman's business. Enough of this talk, let's eat," Betty said sternly.

Betty and Arvin ate mostly in silence with the only interruptions being Arvin's under his breath comments about Dr. Russell's intentions. Betty just ignored his grumblings.

Betty started back to work with Dr. Russell. The next two years went by so quickly. Ruth was getting bigger and loved to go to work with mommy. The twins, Cora and Tommy, would play with her when they got home from school. Betty did feel like part of the family more each day. When Dr. Russell got home, he would sit down with Betty and have a cup of her tea and tell her about the patients he had helped that day. Betty looked forward to this time. Arvin really didn't talk to her about his day, or much at all.

One afternoon when Dr. Russell got home and they were sitting with their tea, he started to tell Betty that the country was preparing to go dry, no more alcohol. She asked why our country would do that, although she didn't really have an opinion.

He said there were many reasons for prohibiting alcohol. However, since it was getting late, decided to put off any further conversation about that until the following week. It was time to get Betty and Ruth home. He realized he looked forward to their "tea and conversation" time together, a little too much. It felt good to come home, sit and share his day with someone. However, this was the wrong someone.

In January 1920, the ratification of the 18th Amendment to the United States Constitution went into effect which banned the manufacture, transportation and sale of intoxicating liquors ushered in a period in American history known as Prohibition. The increase of illegal production and sale of liquor, known as "bootlegging" and the proliferation of speakeasies (illegal drinking spots) was the result. This experiment was introduced due to the national mood in America. When America entered the war in 1917 the national mood also turned against drinking alcohol. It was believed that a ban on alcohol would boost supplies of important grains such as barley. The religious sect believed that the consumption of alcohol went against God's will. And finally, many agreed that it was wrong for some Americans to enjoy alcohol while the country's young men were at war.

By law, any wine or spirits Americans had stashed away in January 1920 were theirs to keep and enjoy in the privacy of their homes. For most, this amounted to only a few bottles. But, some affluent drinkers built cavernous wine cellars and even bought out whole liquor store inventories. Drug stores were allowed to sell "medicinal whiskey" for everything from toothaches to the flu. With a physician's prescription, "patients" could legally buy a pint of hard liquor every ten days. The pharmaceutical booze often came with seemingly laughable doctor's orders such as, "Take three ounces every hour for stimulant until stimulated." Many speakeasies eventually operated under the guise of being pharmacies, and legitimate chains flourished. The people who illegally made, imported, or sold alcohol during this time were called bootleggers.

∽∾

Arvin and his buddies had been stopping off for a few beers after work and now that had come to an end. Needless to say, they were none too happy. They had been discussing what they would do when this day came. The prohibition movement's strength had grown due to the Woman's Christian Temperance Union. Their discussions included how they were going to capitalize on this new situation and where they were going to get their beer. Of course, Arvin had one of his "city dreams" idea. He would wheel, deal, and profit from this situation.

One evening, when Arvin got home, he said in a very loud, excited voice, "Betty, I need to talk with you before we eat."

"Okay, sounds serious," Betty answered.

"It is. Ya know, since we can't buy beer no more, the guys and me have been talkin'-"

Betty interrupted and said, "Is this some of that man's business you've been talkin' about?"

"Betty! Now listen. Each of us is gonna brew beer and sell it," Arvin said emphatically.

"What?' Betty almost screamed, then lowered her voice as not to upset Ruth and continued, "Brew beer? That's gonna get us into jail."

"Stop." Arvin said loudly stomping his foot. "People are gonna want to buy beer to drink at home, aren't they? This is a good time to make some extra money," Arvin said more calmly.

"Arvin, how you gonna make beer when you work all day?" Betty said a little more composed as well.

55

"Well, I thought you could make it the days you aren't with the twins. And since you aren't workin' as much, we could use the extra money."

"What? Now how am I gonna make it here in our place. This isn't Kentucky. Back home people had stills and the stills were big."

"Big pots. A couple of big pots. All we need is some grain, malt syrup, hops, and yeast."

"Arvin, you're not thinkin' straight. This is a crazy idea. It's against the law. We could go to jail. What about Ruth? Is this part of your city dreams?" Betty said all in one breath.

"Betty, stop being so difficult. Lots of people are gonna be doin' this. It'll be exciting."

"Pshaw!" Betty said, waving her hand, and dismissing what Arvin was saying.

⌘

"Mother's in the kitchen washing out the jugs; Sister's in the pantry bottling the suds; Father's in the cellar mixing up the hops; Johnny's on the front porch watching for the cops." This is a poem written by a New York state Rotary Club member during prohibition which seemed to sum up the climate in Chicago during the first 18 months.

⌘

Betty gave in to Arvin's new idea and started baking and stirring the ingredients that produced the beer. Arvin started by selling to his buddies and soon the people in their building were buying, too. Actually, some started helping Betty in exchange for a drink or two. It was becoming quite the enterprise.

One evening while they were eating supper, Arvin cautiously said, "Betty, one of my buddies has a friend who is a cop. He's looking for a place to get a drink now and then and can't go to a speakeasy. My buddy is going to bring him here to get a bottle or two."

"Arvin, a cop? Are ya crazy?" Betty responded in her high voice.

Arvin knew she would respond that way and decided to take the offensive. He said authoritatively, "Betty, my buddy said he's a good guy. Stop worrying. You're always worrin' about somethin' and your worrin' gets on my nerves. I trust my buddy and I know he wouldn't be part of settin' me up."

"One of us has to worry. I guess I do it for both of us. Sorry. Hope you're right about this cop Arvin, and that it isn't a set up." She saw the look on Arvin's face and added, "I know, stop worrin'." Betty gave up. He had won again. Him and his city dreams.

The conversation continued around their bootlegging enterprise.

"Betty, we need more bottles," Arvin said.

"Where did you get all those bottles anyway?" Betty asked.

"From one of the breweries that stopped making brew. They went into making ice cream, I think. All of us guys put up some money and bought a couple of cases of bottles. People have been keepin' them. We'll get more. Just make sure people bring them back."

Arvin did get more bottles and Betty continued making brew. One day, she got a very interesting visitor. As Betty opened the door, she saw a pudgy little man wearing a Stetson style hat that seemed odd on such a small man.

"Mrs. Jamison?" The pudgy little man asked.

"Yes, who are you?" Betty asked.

"I am the owner of this building. My name is David, David Miles. It has come to my attention that beer is being brewed in your apartment. Is that true?" Mr. Miles asked.

"I knew Arvin would get us in trouble with his wild notions. Yes, Mr. Miles, it's true. Are ya gonna turn us in?"

"No Mrs. Jamison. I'm not here to turn you in. I'm here to help. Since there are quite a few of the residents in this building brewing, I thought it might be better for everyone if it was a joint effort. You could use a bigger space, and bigger pots."

Betty stood there with an open mouth and the word "what" escaped through her lips. She could not believe what she was hearing. She thought maybe Arvin was right about luck always being on their side.

The pudgy little man continued, "Because of the position I hold in the city, Mrs. Jamison, I cannot go to a speakeasy. However, I like a suds now and then. I work with a lot of city officials who also would like a place to get their alcohol. So, if I open the basement up to you, get you bigger pots in exchange for being able for us to wet our whistles now and then, would you be willing to do that?"

"Uh, I don't know what to say, Mr. Miles. Guess, it'd be okay. Have to talk to my husband. He's at work now and won't be home until this evening."

"Fine, can I stop back tonight when your husband gets home?" Mr. Miles asked.

"Guess that'd be alright."

Betty couldn't wait until Arvin got home. The whole bootlegging thing had her very nervous. As soon as Arvin walked through the door that evening Betty quickly got his attention by telling him about their visitor.

"Arvin, I got a surprise visit today from the owner of our building, a Mr. David Miles. He came askin' about our home brewing. He-"

Arvin quickly interrupted her, "What, who is he? What did you tell him?"

"He knew what we are doin' and he knows about the other people in our buildin' doin' the same thing. He wants to trade the basement for beer." Betty answered right away.

"What?" Arvin asked almost in Betty's high voice.

"Mr. Miles said he'd open the basement to give us a bigger space to brew in. He even said he'd get us bigger pots."

"What's his angle?" Arvin asked suspiciously.

"Beer." Betty responded and then she said it again, "Beer. Oh

Arvin, I hope you haven't gone and got us into something that is gonna cause us trouble."

"Betty, there you go again, worrin' for nothing," Arvin said.

"Mr. Miles is comin' back tonight to talk with you. Then you can find out more about what he's got in mind. Now, let me get Ruth ready for bed and put her down while you eat your dinner."

Betty was just finishing putting Ruth to bed when she heard Arvin call, "Betty, I believe Mr. Miles is here."

Wondering why he would call her since he was closer to the door, she answered, "Well answer the door."

As Arvin opened the door, he said, "Are you Mr. Miles?"

The pudgy little man answered, "Yes, and I take it that you are Mr. Jamison."

"Ya, Arvin Jamison. Come in. Now what's this about the basement and bigger pots for brewin?"

"Arvin, may I call you Arvin?" Mr. Miles answered with a question of his own.

"Sure," Arvin said.

"Arvin, I am one of the city officials in Chicago and since prohibition, it has been awkward for me to get a suds now and then. I cannot take the chance of a raid at one of the speakeasies. My co-workers are in the same position. So, when it came to my attention that you and Mrs. Jamison have been home brewing for quite some time now, I thought that you could use more room and I could use a beer now and then. The basement does have a furnace room and a coal shoot, but there is plenty of room for you to continue your enterprise. I own the building so I can offer this to you without concern. I understand that there are some others in the building doing the same thing. Is that true?" Mr. Miles asked.

"I suppose. Does that matter?" Asked Arvin.

"Well, I thought all of you could help each other if you had a bigger space and more pots or equipment to brew. The other thing is that the basement has a separate entrance in the back of the building. Right now, you have too many people coming and going in the front of the building. That's how I knew what was going on here. Using the back entrance won't cause any real attention. The door has a lock. No one can just walk in and out and you could set up regular hours for people to come and pick up their brew. So, what do you think?"

Arvin quickly answered, "Mr. Miles, I like the way you think! This set up could really work out for all of us." Then Arvin asked, "Are you wantin' some part of the money that we collect from sellin' our beer?"

"No. All I want is a place where I can get my beer without a lot of risk, or at least, less risk than going to the speakeasies. If it is good with you, I will get a couple of big pots for you and have them put in the basement sometime this week. Good?"

"Good!" Arvin said emphatically.

Mr. Miles kept his word and those big pots plus other brewing equipment showed up in the basement within that week. So, Arvin and Betty were off and running a bigger home bootlegging enterprise. Betty brewed on her four days off from watching the twins. Two of the neighbors brewed on the other three days. Betty brewed during the day and Arvin bottled the brew in the evenings. Things were going good. Their customers were high city officials, cops, and Arvin's buddies from the factory. They were bringing in enough money to pay for expenses and then some. They branched out into making home-distilled hard liquor, which was called "bathtub gin". Arvin discovered that it was actually easier than brewing beer. Several years went by, Betty had another child, Carol, and was no longer working for the doctor. Things were going good for Arvin and Betty.

On February 14, 1929, seven men of the North Side Irish gang were killed by the South Side Italian gang led by one of the most notorious gangsters, Al Capone, during prohibition to take control of the organized crime in Chicago. These murders were given the name the Saint Valentine's Day Massacre. There were raids all over the city. Speakeasies were being hit, closed, and reopened the next day. People turned more and more to criminal activity, organized criminals thrived and most common people looked at them as heroes.

CHAPTER 15
Arvin's Hen House

In 1930, Arvin and Betty were hit with a financial blow. Arvin lost his job. He got laid off during the time that a financial decline was leading the country into an economic downturn, which would lead to the Great Depression. Over the last year, Arvin's hours had been decreasing due to the factories in the garment district receiving less and less orders. Arvin gave Betty the bad news one afternoon when he arrived home.

"Arvin, what are you doing home so early?" Betty asked surprised to see Arvin.

"Betty, got bad news," Arvin answered.

"Oh, dear. What's wrong? Arvin what happened?"

"Lost my job today."

"Oh no. Why?" Betty asked with a worried look.

"The factory has been letting people go every week the last couple of months. All the garment factories are doin' the same thing. Got nowhere to go."

"Arvin, we got the money we've saved from our brewin'. I could find another domestic job, I suppose," Betty said, trying not to show she was worried.

"Maybe, but people are loosin' their jobs all over the city. I'm meetin' up with some of the guys that were let go. We're gonna think about what we can put together."

"Like what?"

"Don't know."

"I sure hope it's not another idea like makin' alcohol," Betty said quickly.

"Brewin' has been good to us. You can't say it hasn't."

"Ya, but I've been doin' most of the work that comes along with it. Brewin', workin' and takin' care of Ruth and Carol is not part of my city dreams, they have been yours. I shouldn't have stopped workin' for Dr. Russell," Betty said in a tired voice.

"Aw, Betty quit your complaining, will ya. Women are supposed to support the man's dream, that's how it's supposed to be."

"Sorry, you're right. I'm just tired, that's all. I know you've worked just as hard at the factory. I've been thinkin' we should look to be quittin' our brewin'. Arvin, we've been lucky with all this crime goin' on, that we have been left alone."

"Betty, we're little guys in the bootleggin' thing. We're no threat."

"Maybe so, but now we can't quit." It's our only way to make some money. Oh, now what are we gonna do?" Betty said despairingly.

Arvin responded somewhat annoyed by Betty's tone of hopelessness, "I told you, stop worrin'. Some of the guys and me are meetin' up. We'll come up with somethin'."

"I know," Betty quickly replied and changed the subject. "By the way, I asked Serena to come over for some tea tomorrow. She's been so busy with the family she works for that we haven't seen each other for a while. Will you be home?"

"No, goin' down to the factory and pick up my pay."

Betty and Arvin continued their discussion about their bootlegging enterprise and if Betty should go back to work as a domestic. Nothing was solved and they decided to go to bed and talk about it another time.

The next morning, Arvin left to meet the guys and Betty

prepared a pot of tea for Serena's visit. Just as she was finishing up in the kitchen Serena knocked on the door. Betty answered the door and was greeted by a great big hug.

"Betty, it is so good to see you!" Serena said as she walked into the hallway.

"It's good to see you, too. Let's go into the kitchen and have some tea," Betty responded.

"That would be nice. Betty, you gotta tell me everything. It's been almost a year since I've seen you. I was starting to worry about you. Is everything okay? How are Ruth and Carol? Are you still working for that doctor?"

"My, oh, my Serena, so many questions," Betty answered laughing a little.

☙❧

While Betty and Serena were catching up on their news, Arvin was having a conversation of his own.

"So, guys, what are we gonna do now that we have no work?" Arvin asked the guys from the factory.

"Arvin, you've been home bootleggin' so you should be okay," Joe said. Joe and Arvin had worked together on the milling machines.

"Ya, but how much longer is this here prohibition gonna last? Have to come up with something else. Something that we can do until the factories put us back to work," Arvin responded.

"Ya, but what?" One of the other guys asked.

"Not sure yet. I have some ideas. One of my ideas is prostitution," Arvin answered.

"Prostitution?" Joe shouted.

"Yes, whores, prostitutes, ladies of the night. Ya know."

"Now, just how are we gonna go about puttin' that idea together? And besides, aren't all the gangsters running the houses?"

"Ya, but mostly they are runnin' the prostitution that goes on in the cabarets or saloons. I'm talkin' about somethin' else, like

64

lookin' into some of the furnished apartments or rooming houses where a lot of young single women live."

"Now, you're going in the right direction. Maybe we go to one of the rooming houses that are being used for prostitution and see if we can work a deal," Joe said.

"What kind of deal?" Arvin asked.

"Don't know yet. Look guys, the king of wheeling and dealing is asking us what kind of deal," Joe said.

"What about Betty? Will she be okay with this?" One of the other guys asked.

"No, of course not. She is so dang prudish," Arvin answered.

Joe quickly said, "But she did go along with the bootleggin' idea. And you told me she has done most of the brewin'."

"You're right. She's nice enough, but I'm bored. Not sure if I'm bored with her or with my lifestyle. Workin' at the factory six days a week, being nagged if I stop off for a few beers with you guys, responsibilities with the girls and then there's the juggin'. Just doesn't seem like city dreams to me," Arvin said.

"You got a good woman there. She certainly is a hard worker herself," Joe responded.

I know, just thinkin' out loud. Maybe checkin' out this prostitution thing will give me some excitement. Let's go get our pay," Arvin said and motioned to the guys to follow.

❦

Back at the apartment, Betty and Serena were still having tea and catching up. They had been talking about the violence and crime going on in the city.

"With all the killin's goin' on here in this city our brewin' days may be comin' to an end. Sometimes, I get so afraid for me and the girls. The shootin's are getting' closer to us. Carol was playing outside with her dolls when a man ran up to her, squatted down like he was hidin' or usin' her to shield him. A car drove by like they were lookin' for somethin' or someone. I was sittin' on the stoop outside watchin' and my heart stopped 'cause I saw the front of a gun stickin' out the car window. When the car past the man got up and ran in the opposite direction," Betty said.

Serena gasped and said, "Betty, I'm so sorry. Did Carol know what "happened?"

"No, she just thought the man wanted to play. Thank goodness Ruth was in school. I worry about her, too. Ruth is eleven now and knows what's goin' on in the city and what we're doin' in the basement. She knows not to say anything but she is still a child. Here I am goin' on about me. Tell me more about what has been going on with you."

"Well, you know the family I am working for?" Serena asked.

"Ya."

"Well, they moved to what is called the North Shore in a town called Northbrook. It seems so far away. However, it is a small pretty place, not too many people and not much hustle and bustle. So, now I live with them."

"Sounds so nice. Do you like living with them?"

"Actually, I love it. As you know, living in the settlement house wasn't very private and not much room. So, now I have my own room with a private bathroom."

"I'm so happy for you! How did you get here today?"

"The wife was coming into the city. She drove me."

"They have an automobile?" Betty asked in a surprised voice.

"Yes."

"Someday I hope Arvin and me get one of those automobiles. Sometimes I wonder what's next for us. What's next for me? Arvin and his city dreams."

"Betty, what are your dreams?"

"Serena, I don't really know. Never thought about it. Back home, I was so busy helpin' momma with the kids and farm chores and such that there was no time to think about other things. Since Arvin and me been here in Chicago, all I've done is work. I loved workin' with the twins. Dr. Russell was good to me, and to us. Why, he even stopped by after Ruth was born and brought things for our new place here."

"Betty, I told you he was sweet on you."

"Serena, don't be silly. I worked for him is all." Betty answered, slightly red in the face.

"Did you ever think to flirt back with him?"

"Serena, that wouldn't be right. Although, I sure enjoyed the times we would sit, have tea and talk."

"When did you and Dr. Russell sit and drink tea together?" Serena asked with surprise.

"Dr. Russell and me would visit with each other for a spell after he came home from the hospital. I was lookin' forward to that time a bit too much though. Our tea times lessened. By the time I left his employ, we hardly talked at all. I believe he was feelin' the same way and backed off our times together."

"Your life with him would be a whole lot easier than what you have been doing with Arvin."

"I married Arvin for better or worse."

"It seems to me that you got more of the worse than the better. Cleaning, cooking, taking care of Dr. Russell's twins then coming home and start brewing because of Arvin's city dreams, and having babies in between. Betty, I would like to see you not work so hard."

"You gotta do what's in front of you. I just take care of what needs to be done."

Betty and Serena continued their conversation and enjoying their tea while Arvin was out making deals. One of the guys from the factory gave Arvin a heads up on a lady who was running a house of prostitution and wanted out of the business. Arvin didn't waste any time in checking it out. He hopped on a trolley and was off on another journey toward his city dreams.

He was tingling with excitement as he walked up the stairs of the typical Chicago style two story building. His excitement got the best of him and he started knocking on the door a bit too hard.

He realized that when he heard a voice yell, "Stop banging on the door. I hear you. I'm coming."

As soon as the door opened Arvin started talking, "I understand that you're gettin' out of the business. Is that true?"

The woman who opened the door said, "My, you're direct aren't you? First of all, who are you. How do you know what you know?"

Arvin realized his inappropriateness and replied, slightly embarrassed, "I'm sorry ma'am. My name is Arvin, Arvin Jamison. One of the guys that I worked with at the garment factory frequents your establishment. He told me he overheard a conversation that indicated you wanted to get out of the biz."

"Why would he give you this information?"

"He knew I was tryin' to figure out how to get into the prostitution business," Arvin quickly responded, still a bit uneasy.

"Why? I'm getting' out because of the mob's involvement in prostitution and their intimidating way of demanding a percentage of what the girls make. It is becoming dangerous to be in this business unless you are part of the "in group", the mob. Even then, they are killing their own, fighting for their territories. It has become too much for me. So, again, I ask you why?"

"May I come in and continue our talk inside. I feel awkward standing outside in the doorway."

The lady opened the door and motioned to him to follow her. They entered a side room and the lady motioned for him to sit on one of the two chairs.

Arvin continued with the conversation, "I just got laid off and don't mind taking risks. My wife and I have been bootleggin' for several years and have done good with it. We brew for a lot of high officials and cops. So, I'm thinkin' this here prohibition isn't gonna last forever, so, I need and want somethin' else to make money and give me some excitement, too. Can we talk about this?"

"Hey, slow down. You didn't even ask my name. How do you know I'm the owner? I could be a plant by vice. Gotta be more careful if you want to get into this business."

"I know your name is Lori. The guy that told me about ya, told me your name. Sorry, I called you, ma'am. I should've taken the time to get proper introductions instead of bargin' right into my talk. I'm just so excited," Arvin quickly responded.

"Okay Arvin, then let's talk business and see if you have what it takes to run a place like mine. I also want to get to know you better."

Arvin and Lori came to an agreement. Lori had been paying the rent and running the business. She was burned out. She didn't want to deal with the men and live in fear of the mob. She was through with the business, but did need a place to live. Arvin would manage the girls and collect the money. Lori would live rent free. The average clerk in Chicago earned $6.67 a week. The prostitutes could earn $30 to $50 a week. Arvin just knew he made the right deal. Now to deal with Betty.

Arvin planned out what he was going to tell Betty. He had to lie to her. He had never lied to her before, but he knew he couldn't tell her about his prostitution business. Bootlegging was one thing, but running a whore house was another. All the way home he practiced what he was going to say to her. The trolley stopped and he got off. Now it was time to see how well he had practiced, since he was home.

"Betty, we got us some good luck. I go back to work a couple hours a week. A short week," Arvin explained excitedly.

"How did that happen?" Betty asked in her surprised voice.

"Went to get my pay and the boss asked me. Guess they have some small orders comin' in," he felt his face get flushed from lying and feared Betty would catch on.

"Oh Arvin, that is good luck. Did any of the other fellas that got laid off get hired back for a short week?"

"Just a couple of us," Arvin replied. He was relieved Betty didn't catch on to his lie.

"I'm so glad since it's gettin' hard to get what we need to brew as well as other food supplies. They are startin' to ration things and I understand things are goin' to get worse. At least we have a little luck with you gettin' some of your job back. We were startin' to get ahead, thinkin' of gettin' a bigger place and now that doesn't seem possible. Ruth and Carol are gettin' too old to be sleepin' in the parlor." Betty continued talking however, she stopped when she realized Arvin wasn't listening and was walking away. "Where ya goin'?"

Arvin answered as he was walking toward the door, "Goin' to meet the guys to see if any more of them got short hours. See ya later."

With that, Arvin left Betty and just couldn't wait to get back to his new business. He felt a little guilty for lying to Betty, but quickly got past it when he got to Lori's.

"Mr. Jamison, back so soon? Here to check out your merchandise?" Lori said, as she opened the door.

"I thought I'd complete our deal. Had to leave earlier to take care of somethin'. Never thought about checkin' out the merch. Not a bad idea though...and call me Arvin."

Lori said, smiling, "Come on, I'll show you around the whole place this time, Arvin."

Lori's place was built in the early 1900's and was Chicago's version of the New York brownstone. The lime stone façade was harvested primarily from quarries around a city in Indiana and was built as a two story multi-family building. Lori lived on the second floor sharing it with one other woman and the business was held on the first floor, which housed a kitchen, dining room, parlor, two bedrooms and bathroom. The dining room and parlor had been turned into boudoirs. Lori's place was the same layout with the dining room and parlor intact. Solid oak wood covered all the floors with lush floor rugs strewn about. The rugs kept the warmth in and the noise out.

"Come meet the girls," Lori said, as she motioned for Arvin to follow her.

As they entered the kitchen they came upon a girl sitting at a table drinking a cup of coffee. Lori approached her and said, "Nellie, meet Mr. Jamison, your new boss."

"Howdy," Nellie replied.

"Hi Nellie," Arvin responded.

"Nellie moved to Chicago from Tennessee and has been with me for seven months," Lori said.

Nellie was a big girl, about 5' foot 8", dusty blonde hair, and very curvaceous. Her southern charm won over even the shyest of men.

"Lori, when did you decide to get out of the biz?" Nellie asked.

"I have been thinking about it for a while now. Just didn't know how to get out and still make a living. Mr. Jamison and I worked out a deal. I'll be living upstairs, but Mr. Jamison will be conducting all the business with you girls," Lori explained.

"Well, Mr. Jamison, welcome to our hen house," Nellie said with a smile.

"Thanks, lookin' forward to collectin' the eggs," Arvin said and gave a chuckle.

Arvin went on to meet Lillian. A French woman who was petite in stature, long black hair and blue eyes that looked like marbles. Dolly, who was a feisty Italian, also on the petite side with long brown wavy hair and green eyes. Ginger, who was an Irish gal, porcelain skin, full figured and curvy. Last but not least, Ruby, a robust girl who was from a farm in Indiana.

Lori and Arvin went over how he needed to book his girls. The procedure was easy enough. Clients never gave their right name and all paid in cash. Someone comes around to collect "protection money" once a week and that was something that Arvin knew he needed to work out. Until then, he would just enjoy his new enterprise. Arvin bid everyone goodbye and headed home.

CHAPTER 16

Another New Beginning

Mr. Miles, owner of the building, was just about to knock on the door when Arvin walked up.

"Mr. Miles, is there anythin' wrong?" Arvin asked with surprise.

"No, just stopped by to talk with you and your wife about moving," Mr. Miles answered.

"Movin?" Arvin asked quickly.

"Yes, I have an apartment that came empty that is bigger than yours and I need your apartment for my niece. Let me explain. You see, my niece is in a wheelchair. Since your apartment is on the first floor, she could get in and out on her own. I would be willing to give you the other apartment, which is on the second floor for the same rent. It has two bedrooms and I thought you wouldn't mind giving up your apartment since you could use the extra room." He continued talking as he noticed the puzzled look on Arvin's face, "I know it's an inconvenience. However, nothing with our basement enterprise changes. Do you think your wife will be okay with moving?"

Arvin collected his thoughts and the wheeler dealer in him realized that this was a great deal and said, "Ya, sure, we can move."

"Shouldn't we go in and talk with your wife? After all, she's got some say in this, too?" Mr. Miles asked.

"Betty goes along with what I say. Just when do you need us to make the move?"

"I know this is so much to ask, but could you and your family move upstairs by next week?"

Arvin answered quickly not wanting the deal to go south, "Sure, I will tell Betty."

Mr. Miles said, with a sigh of relief, "I am very grateful. Here is the key to the apartment upstairs, it is already cleaned out and scrubbed down. Now, what do you say about having a suds?"

"Sure, meet you downstairs," Arvin answered and walked into his apartment.

Arvin called out to Betty, "Betty, where are you?" Just then Betty walked out of their bedroom into the kitchen. Arvin continued talking, "Just met Mr. Miles outside and I have some good news...more good luck for us."

"Oh, Arvin, come sit down and have your supper. Now what's this good luck?" Betty asked.

"He's givin' us another apartment with two bedrooms upstairs." Arvin said excitedly.

"How, why?"

"Something about needin' our place for his niece who's in a wheelchair and needs a first floor place to live. He wants us to move by next week. I told him that we would."

"Without askin' me?" Betty said quickly.

"No need. I knew you would love a bigger place," Arvin answered authoritatively.

"That's not the point, Arvin. We used to talk things over and make decisions together," Betty said feeling a bit hurt.

"I'm goin' downstairs to meet him for some suds. I don't want to be standin' here bein' nagged at, when I brought you good news."

"Sorry. Of course, I'm happy. Guess we're movin' next week. I'll tell Carol and Ruth, they'll be happy. Don't be gone too long, don't want your supper to get cold."

Arvin waved his hand in acknowledgement and left to have a suds.

Betty and Arvin settled into their new place with Ruth and Carol. Since it was considerably bigger, the girls got their own room and Betty and Arvin once again had their privacy. Instead of three rooms, they now had five, an additional bedroom, and a formal dining room that was between the kitchen and parlor. Things started to look up for Arvin and Betty, once again.

One evening when they were sitting in the parlor Arvin said, "Betty, our city dreams are comin' true. I got my job back, even though it's only short hours, and now we got us here this new bigger place to live. Luck is sure is comin' our way again."

"Ya, you're right Arvin, but remember, this here city dreams thing is yours, not mine. Raisin' these girls, while home brewin' hasn't been easy. Now that we have ourselves a bigger place, and Ruth and Carol are both in school, I'm gonna get me some work. Maybe take in ironin' or sewin' to bring in some money. Or, even get me some other domestic work, even if it is, as you put it, short hours." Betty said.

"Good idea. You could work more hours if you want. Since I'm workin' short hours I can do more of the brewin'. Some of the guys at the factory told me that a lot of the home brewin' places are bein' raided and shut down by the cops. We sure have luck that some of the cops come to us for their brew and havin' some of those highfalutin city guys, too."

"Well, we better be watchin' careful and not get too cocky. I'll go over to the agency tomorrow after the girls go to school and see what they got."

"Good. Now let's have some of your fine cookin' in our dining room and celebrate this here new place."

୬୦ଏ

The morning after Ruth and Carol left for school, Betty and Arvin left to go their separate ways. Betty on her way to the agency and Arvin on his way to Lori's. Both were on a mission.

Lori was surprised to see Arvin at her door and said, "Well, Mr. Jamison, Arvin, you're here kind of early. Come on in and have some coffee. We can finalize all of the details of our deal."

Arvin eagerly responded, "Okay, don't mind if I do." Arvin took a seat as Lori poured him a cup. He took a sip and said, "Good coffee."

"Thanks. Would you like something to eat?"

"Nah, had me somethin' at home. Betty made me some biscuits and gravy."

"Your wife, is she a good cook?"

"Ya, her best cookin' is fried chicken. Nothin' like it."

"What did she say about our business deal?"

"I didn't tell her."

"What?" Lori exclaimed.

"I didn't tell her. She wouldn't understand my wantin' to do this. She would be naggin' at me, and I hate her naggin'."

"How is this going to work?"

"I told her that I was hired back by the factory on short hours. She won't suspect anything, especially since I will be bringin' home cash. She'll just think I cashed my check on the way home from work. Got it covered," Arvin said smugly.

"Sounds like it. Okay, since you met all of the girls, let's go over the books that I keep. I keep them pretty much for me, so I know how much I bring in and how much I need to pay the girls. I usually pay them at the end of their day, in cash, just to keep things simple. You can do it differently if you want. The one thing you do want to do for sure, is to keep the names of your clients, for insurance, if you get what I mean?"

"I do. Can I see the list?"

"Of course!"

As Arvin was perusing the list he exclaimed, "There are names on this list of cops that come by my place for their alcohol-"

Lori interrupted saying, "That is good protection for you."

"...and look here, names of city officials that also come by my place. City dreams comin' true."

"What?"

"Just somethin' I say. I've always had city dreams. I never knew what that meant until now. Lori, I think we are gonna make a good team."

"Arvin, I'm out of the business, remember. That's why you're here."

"Ya, I know, but, since you're gonna be livin' upstairs, I hope I can come up for a cup of coffee now and then."

Lori responded, smiling seductively, "Anytime Arvin, anytime! Now, let's have another cup of coffee."

Arvin caught that smile and responded, "Sure thing."

Arvin and Lori were enjoying their coffee when all of a sudden, they heard heavy pounding at the door. Lori got up to answer, but Arvin stopped her and told her that since it was his business now, he would answer the door...and he did.

However, before the door was all the way open a man put his foot in the door and asked, "Where's the lady that runs this place."

Arvin opened the door a little farther. As the man was trying to step inside, Arvin said, "She no longer runs this place, I do." Then Arvin asked sternly, while blocking the man from coming inside, "Who are you?"

"It doesn't matter who I am. What matters is I'm here to collect my money," the man answered.

"What money?" Arvin asked in the same authoritative voice the man had displayed.

"Fee for protection," the man answered boldly.

"Fee for protection? Protection from what?"

"Listen Mr., don't get smart with me. I don't know who you are, but you'd better get my money," the man said shaking his finger in Arvin's face.

Just then Lori called out, "Arvin, is there a problem?"

Hearing Lori, the man with the shaking finger yelled back, "Hey lady, I'm here to collect."

Lori walked over to Arvin and said, "Arvin, this is the guy that I was telling you about."

Arvin turned and looked at Lori and asked, "Why have you paid him?"

"He threatened me," Lori answered.

The man interrupted them, saying, "Hey, you guys can have your chatty party later. Right now, I want the money."

Arvin turned back to the man and said sternly, "No, no more money for protection. Don't need it."

"You know what I will do to you, if you don't pay?" The man responded with a threat.

"Not worried," Arvin responded pushing the man back through the door. "Now get out. We have some customers comin' from the city, and I'm sure you've run into them before. They'd love to know about this shakedown. Now leave."

The man threatened Arvin again as he turned "You'll wish you had paid."

While Arvin was having his first "business meeting" Betty was at the agency having one of her own.

CHAPTER 17

Three Boys, Lions and Tigers

Betty walked into the agency and approached the lady sitting at the desk. "Good mornin', is Marie here?" Betty asked.

The lady responded, "No, she hasn't been here for over seven years. My name is Elaine, how can I help you?"

"My name is Betty and she got me a job many years ago when I first came to this city. I'm now lookin' to get another domestic job. I cooked for Dr. Russell and his twins for years. I'm sure he would give me a good reference. He worked at Mercy hospital," Betty said anxiously.

"Betty what is your full name?" Elaine asked.

"Betty Jamison."

"Our files don't go back, but five years. So, I have to ask you to fill out this paperwork. I am sure things changed for you anyway."

"Yes, they have. I'll be glad to fill this out. Just as long as I can get me some work."

"I'm sure we will have something for you. I'll look while you finish the paperwork."

Betty nodded, smiled and continued to finish filling out the paperwork.

Elaine was thumbing through her files when she stopped and said, "Mrs. Jamison, I do have something in our Northshore district, in a town called Northbrook. Now, it is far, however, there is a train that goes out that way."

"My friend Serena lives with a family in Northbrook. She said it's kinda far. If you have anything closer, that would be better. If not, then I'll listen about Northbrook."

Elaine went through some of the papers on her desk and offered Betty another option. "I have a family in the Lincoln Park area, near the zoo, who needs someone to watch their three children. Three young children, two, three and four years old. I've had this request for quite some time. Can't seem to get someone to take on these three children."

"Elaine, I can do it. I practically raised my brothers and sisters and I have two children of my own. The Lincoln Park area will be easier for me to get to than Northbrook. Tell me more about these children."

Elaine reads from one of the papers and said, "Let me see. They are all boys. Johnny, Eddie and Jimmy. Jimmy is the oldest and Johnny is the baby. Mr. Altman works out of town and is home on the weekends. Mrs. Altman wants help with the boys. I'm not sure if cooking is part of the duties or not. Are you interested in this family?"

"Yes I am. When can I start?" Betty, excited, answered quickly.

"Right after we get your references from Dr. Russell. That shouldn't take too long if he still works at Mercy Hospital. Do you have a telephone?"

"Yes, we just got one. I put our number down on the paper I filled out."

"Good, we will call you as soon as we get in touch with Dr. Russell."

"Thank you, Elaine. I'll be waiting for your call."

Betty left hoping she'd hear from Elaine soon. She knew that Dr. Russell would give her good references, if Elaine could find him. Her mind went to the twins and reflected on the first day she met them. She could feel flutters in her heart when thinking about when Dr. Russell told her that she was part of their family. So much time has passed since then. She is not that naïve 18-year-old girl from Kentucky any more. Her thoughts moved to what she would make for dinner now that she was approaching their apartment.

When she got home, Arvin was sitting at the kitchen table. Betty surprised said, "Arvin, you're home early."

"Yes, my day was short. I will be workin' every day, but short hours. Did the agency have somethin' for you?"

Before Betty could answer Arvin, the telephone rang. Betty hung up the phone and told Arvin about her conversation at the agency.

"That was the call to tell me that I got the job with a family takin' care of three little boys. That was fast. The agency called Dr. Russell and he told them that I was a good loyal worker. I'm glad that the agency got a hold of him so quick, and I'm glad you're workin' short hours so you'll be here when Carol gets home from school."

"Betty what about the brewin'? When will you do that?"

"Arvin, I'll cut our brewin' days to the weekends. Some of our customers have gone into business for themselves anyway. Most of our customers are those cop friends of yours and the high falutin' city officials. I'd like to stop brewin' altogether," Betty responded tersely.

Arvin didn't respond. Betty prepared and made super in silence. They ate the same way.

Arvin went on deceiving Betty, and Betty went to work every day taking care of Johnny, Eddie and Jimmy. Their brewing was winding down since there was talk about Prohibition coming to an end. People like Betty and Arvin had been running illegal alcohol operations and some of these people had plenty of money with which to pay bribes. Because there were few federal agents, and because local police were easily bribed, the illegal operations couldn't completely be stopped. Cops frequented individuals like Betty and Arvin or kept what they confiscated from their raids for their drink.

⌘

Due to the tremendous rise of organized crime, Prohibition failed and came to an end just before Christmas in 1933. By 1933, when the Great Depression reached its lowest point, some 13 to 15 million Americans were unemployed and nearly half of the country's banks had failed. Chicago was one of the hardest hit cities due to the city's dependence on manufacturing.

⌘

Arvin's business was flourishing. He went from selling alcohol to selling sex. Some of the cops he was serving his home brew to came to his new place of business for a little recreation from time to time. He had built in protection from being raided. Lori and Arvin were getting along very well, too well. He did not sample the wares of his girls. However, Lori got more than free rent from Arvin.

During one of Arvin's early morning coffees with Lori, she asked, "Arvin, does your wife suspect that you're fooling around on her?"

"No. She is so into the three little boys she's taking care of and too tired to pay attention to anything when she gets home. She makes supper, we all eat, the girls clean up, then she spends time doin' whatever she does," Arvin responded casually.

"What about your girls?"

"Ruth is always out with her boyfriend and Carol spends time helpin' her mom with whatever they do. Don't see much of either girl."

"It sounds like you don't want to."

"Lori, the truth be known, I don't. I'm not sure kids were part of my city dreams," Arvin said shrugging his shoulders.

"Was I?" Lori asked with that seductive smile.

"I'm sure you were, only with me not knowin'. But I'm sure glad I know now. Why don't you come to my place tomorrow, girls are in school and Betty is workin'?"

"Why? You getting tired of being here so much?"

"Nah, that's not the reason. I just thought it'd be good to have a change of scenery, that's all. Plus, you'd get out of this house for a while."

"Well, I just might take you up on your offer. I'd like to see how the respectable folk live."

"Respectable? Huh! We've been bootleggin' since the beginnin' of Prohibition and now I'm in the hen house business. I'm not sure that would be considered by some folks as respectable," Arvin laughed.

The next day, as usual, Ruth and Carol left for school, Arvin left pretending to go to work and Betty left to take care of the boys. However, this day was different. Arvin came right back to get prepared for Lori's visit for he knew she would come. Since Arvin was on short hours at the factory, it wouldn't be odd for him to be home. It could appear there was no work that day. Bases covered. Lori did show up as Arvin suspected.

When Arvin opened the door, he said, "I knew you would come."

"Sure of yourself, aren't you?" Lori said.

"Just hopin' that's all," Arvin said with a chuckle.

"So, this is your place. Not bad. Your wife has done a good job with it," Lori said as she looked around.

"Ya, she keeps things simple, like she is."

"Where did she do all the bootlegging? This kitchen isn't big enough to handle all the customers you said you had."

"The owner gave us some space in the basement in exchange for brew. Sweet deal. Come'n, let me show you all the rooms, one in particular I think you'll like the best."

Betty was enjoying Johnny, Eddie and Jimmy and from time to time would walk them to the zoo. The boys loved the roaring lions and tigers. They would squeal and run when any one of the big cats roared. Betty avoided the reptile house since they scared her. They brought back memories of her being chased by that big black snake in Kentucky. She missed her home in the hills, her family, but not those snakes.

Monkeys were her favorite. She loved watching them jump and swing from bar to bar. They represented her life. They swung from bar to bar and were free to climb and jump, yet they were still in a cage. Betty felt that way. She was free, alright. Free to watch other people's children, free to raise her own, alone, free to bootleg for her husband, and free to take care of their home, all in the confinement of a life that was designed by her husband. Arvin and his city dreams. His city dream was her cage.

Just on the other side of the zoo were beautiful gardens. As Betty sat enjoying the flowers while the boys ran around and climbed on the statue of Abraham Lincoln, she could feel tears rolling down her cheeks. The boys were too busy to notice. She had been holding in those tears for a while now. Her thoughts were all over the place. Her internal dialog was causing more tears. *Arvin was seldom home. What did he do with his time? He said he was working short hours. Was he hanging out with his men friends? Ruth and Carol don't even know him. He doesn't know them. I love him, however, was this her life? No, she was sure it wasn't. I'm living in his city dream. Where was her dream? What was her dream? Was she to be fulfilled watching other people's children? It wasn't bootlegging, that was for certain. Hush Betty, this is what a wife does, supports her husband. So, stop your complaining.* Just as she wiped away the last tear one of the boys called her name.

"Hey Mrs. Jamison, can we walk back into the zoo now? We want to see the lions and tigers one more time," Johnny asked.

"Okay, Johnny, then we need to get back home. Your momma is gonna have supper ready soon."

As she walked back through the zoo, memories of being with

Ruth and Carol flooded in. Ruth never really took to the zoo much, but Carol loved it. She loved looking at the giraffes with their long necks and the elephants with their long noses. Carol always wanted to know how long did it take for the food to get down the giraffe's neck. She loved throwing peanuts to the elephants and watching them pick them up with their long noses. Betty thought, *she is already 10 years old. Where did the time go? Where did all my time go?* Once again, Betty's thoughts were interrupted. This time by the roaring of one of the big cats and the squeals of the boys. Betty called out to the boys, "Come on now, time to be gettin' home."

Ruth was now 18 years old and didn't get along with her mom all that well. One of the reasons for the current dissension was Carol. Ruth had to take care of Carol until Betty got home from watching the boys. Even though Betty got home earlier these days, Ruth resented her and the time she had to give up watching her sister. Ruth was about to graduate from high school and was already getting excited about being on her own. Betty made Ruth take Carol with her when she went out with her friends, and that was another reason she didn't like her mom.

Ruth and her mom never really had a good relationship. There was always a strain between them, even when she was a young girl. She did not hold to her mother's values of helping out with younger siblings.

CHAPTER 18

Who's That Knocking on My Door?

While Betty was with the boys at the zoo, and Lori was with Arvin at their apartment, Carol was being sent home from school by the nurse.

"Carol, now you take this note home to your momma and have her sign it. Remember, she has to sign it or you can't come back to school. Understand?" The nurse asked.

"Yes, ma'am," Carol answered politely.

"Now go straight home and get into bed. We can't have any of the other children getting sick."

"Yes, ma'am," once again Carol answered politely.

Due to the fear of poliomyelitis, polio, when Carol complained of a headache, she was immediately sent home. Polio was a plague. One day a child had a headache and an hour later that child was paralyzed. How far the virus crept up the spine determined whether he or she could walk afterward or even breathe. Schools were on alert for children getting sick and parents waited breathlessly to see if their child was next to be stricken.

Carol was used to coming home before her mom or Ruth. So, as usual, she went to the kitchen, poured herself a glass of milk. As she was about to sit down, she heard something in her mom and dad's bedroom. Thinking her mom might have come home early, she knocked lightly and then opened the door of the bedroom. As it opened, a loud voice spoke out startling Carol.

"Hey, who's that?" The loud voice yelled.

"Dad? Is that you?" Carol asked surprised. She quickly noticed he wasn't alone and asked, "Who is that lady?"

"Never mind. Get out and shut the door...and you better not say anything to your ma about this or, well you know," Arvin yelled.

Carol shut the door, retreated to her room, and plopped herself on the bed. This wasn't the first time she saw her father with another woman. But, it was the first time she saw another woman in her mom's bed. She just started to cry and cried until she fell asleep. Carol slept all afternoon. She was unaware of her dad and Lori leaving or Ruth and her mom getting home.

Ruth found Carol sleeping and while shaking, she said, "Carol get up. Momma's got supper on the table. What's wrong with you anyway? I've been tryin' to get you up for a long time."

"I got sick at school and they sent me home," Carol replied, still half asleep.

"Well get up and come to the table," Ruth said sharply.

"Ruth something terrible happened," Carol said, stopping Ruth from leaving the room.

"Oh, you and your stories. Hush, come on now."

"Ruth listen to me. I saw pa with another lady today."

"So. Pa knows lots of women, you know that."

"This lady was in momma's bed with Pa," Carol blurted out.

"What? Why would you make something up like that?"

"Ruth, I'm not making it up. Please, listen to me. When I came home, I went into the kitchen and got some milk. While I was drinking my milk, I heard something in momma's and pa's room. I thought maybe momma came home because she wasn't feeling well either. But when I opened the door, there was pa in bed with another lady."

For a moment Ruth stared at Carol in disbelief, then said, "No!"

"Yes!"

"What did you do, say?"

"I didn't say anything. Pa told me to get out, shut the door and don't say anything about this to your ma, or, you know what."

"Carol, are you going to tell momma?"

"I don't know. It'll make her sad. She'll cry. I hate it when she cries. She cries a lot lately."

"I didn't know that," Ruth said surprised.

"Sometimes when you're out with your friends and pa leaves to meet his men friends, she'll sit and cry," Carol said with a sad voice.

"I didn't know, you never told me."

"Sorry."

"Carol, I do think she needs to know."

"Ya, you're right. Will you be with me when I tell her?"

"Yes, but let's pick a time when pa is not around, okay?"

"Okay," Carol agreed.

⟡

In the meantime, Lori and Arvin are back at her apartment and his new business.

"Arvin, that was sure embarrassing. What was I thinking coming to your place?" Lori said, questioning her judgement.

"Sorry, I didn't expect one of the girls comin' home so early," Arvin said.

"I don't think your happy home is going to be as happy as it was once, if your girl tells your wife."

"It's been a long time comin'. Betty hasn't been happy with me for a long time. She suspects my comin's and goin's aren't about workin' at the factory. She just hasn't said anything. We see less of each other even though she gets home earlier than before. I'm supposed to be on short hours at the factory. I should be home early, but I don't always go home."

"Where do you go? You don't come here every day," Lori asked with questioning eyes.

"Out and about. Meet up with the guys. Workin' on deals."

"I would think you have enough to do with this house. Money is really comin' in for you since you serve alcohol now. What a smart idea you had there."

"I had built in customers. Our home brewin' turned this house into a gold mine. I knew my customers could go out publicly to get their drink, but here they can have their drink and then some. The girls are really bringin' in more than ever." Then Arvin asked, "Are you sorry that you gave up this biz?"

"No, not even for a minute. I have a place to live, food on my table, a good man in my bed and freedom. Now, let's get back to Betty. What do you think is going to happen with you two?"

"I'll know when I get back home, if Carol tells her. Gonna leave now and see what's a waitin' for me."

"Take care. Hope you have a good night," Lori said as she kissed him goodbye.

"Thanks. I hope so, too," Arvin replied and with that he turned and left.

❧

When Arvin got home the girls were in their room, and Betty was sitting at the kitchen table sipping a cup of tea.

Betty looked up and said, "Arvin, come in and have something to eat."

"I ate with a couple of buddies on my way home from work,"

Arvin replied.

"Well then, come and have a piece of pie. Made it fresh this morning."

"Sounds good. Betty, you sure can cook."

They sat in silence until he finished his tea and pie. Arvin said he was tired and was going to bed early. Betty got that feeling again of being left out. She poured herself another cup of tea, went into the parlor, sat on their sofa and looked out the window at all of the city's lights. She got lost in them. How beautiful she thought. Just like diamonds. This is Arvin's city dreams. She wondered what her dreams were. She had never taken the time to really think about that. In fact, she wasn't sure she knew how. She decided to go to bed before her feelings took her to a place that was uncomfortable.

❦

The next morning Betty was feeling a little better, but still felt a little left out of Arvin's life. She set the table and called the girls.

"Girls, breakfast is on the table. Come eat, then get ready for church," Betty said.

"Yes, momma," the girls responded in unison.

"Momma, where's pa?" Ruth asked as she sat down to the table.

"He's downstairs in the basement gettin' rid of the last of the brewin' equipment. Prohibition ended last year, but we just didn't get around to cleanin' all that stuff out. Your pa will be right up for breakfast," Betty replied.

"Momma, I want, we want to talk with you later today...alone," Carol said.

"What is it girls?" Betty asked.

Before either one could answer, Arvin came up from the basement.

"All the equipment is now gone. No more bootleggin'. Now, let's have some of that good smellin' grub," Arvin announced.

"Yes, let's all eat. Afterwards, off to church," Betty replied.

On the way home Ruth and Carol listened to their mom talking to their pa.

"It's so nice to have us all together. No more workin' six days a week, no more home brewin' and Arvin, I really like your short hour schedule. It's nice to have you home. Although, lately, haven't seen you much. Out with your men friends, cooking' up some more of your city dreams?" Betty asked.

"Nah. Just hangin' out with them. Get a few beers, you know," Arvin answered.

"Arvin, would you take me to a movie tonight?"

"I have to take care of some business tonight. Maybe the girls would like to go with you."

"What kind of business?"

"Now Betty, you know I take care of the man's business in our family, and this is man's business."

"Seems to me, you got a whole lot of man's business to take care of lately," Betty quickly responded with a slightly sarcastic tone.

"Ya, I do!" Arvin responded in the same tone.

"At least we all got to go to church as a family this morning," Betty said with a softened tone.

As soon as they got home, Arvin said, "Betty, gotta go. See ya later."

That afternoon Betty and the girls caught up with their sewing. While sewing, they chit chatted about the weather, school, the three boys Betty was taking care of and about Ruth's new boyfriend. Time flew by for it had gotten dark already. Neither girl even noticed that Betty got up and warmed up the pot roast they had the night before.

Ruth and Carol were still sewing when they heard their mom say, "Girls set the table, please. Sorry, we are eating so late. I just got caught up in our sewing and conversation. It's nice when we're all together. That doesn't happen very much anymore. Me workin', you both goin' to school and now Ruth, you have new boyfriend."

"Momma, can we talk with you now?" Carol and Ruth said

almost in unison.

"Yes girls. Let's clean up the dishes and talk over some tea and desert. I got some real nice pastries."

The girls agreed and cleaned up while Betty made the tea and put out the pastries.

"Momma, Carol has something to tell you," Ruth said as they all sat down at the table.

"What is it girl?" Betty asked.

Carol told her mom how she got sick at school, and was sent home immediately. Then, she went on to tell her mom how she went into the kitchen to get a glass of milk and heard a noise in their bedroom. When she got to the part of opening the door and what she heard and saw, she busted out into tears. So did her mom. Ruth just sat in silence, unable to emote.

"Carol, I'm so sorry you saw your pa that way. That must've been very hard for you to tell me. Now, don't worry about this. It ain't nothin'. Your pa and I will talk tomorrow. Right now, I feel like I want to go to that movie. I guess I want to be alone," Betty said as she was wiping away her tears.

"Momma, are you sure? What movie house are you going to?" Ruth asked.

"Ya, I'm sure. The other day when I was walkin' with the boys to the zoo, I saw a movie playin' at the Biograph Theater on Lincoln Avenue," Betty said.

"Momma, that's a long walk," Ruth responded.

"I know, but I need to think and besides, I'll be able to sit and rest when I get there. Now, don't worry, get yourselves cleaned up and ready for school tomorrow. I'll be home late," Betty replied.

CHAPTER 19

Bang! Bang!

Betty did take that walk. She walked and walked and walked. Tears came and went and came back again. Her heart was aching. She knew something was wrong. She even thought it might be another woman, but then again had convinced herself that was a crazy thought.

She finally reached the Biograph Theater. When she stepped up to get a ticket the lady told her that the movie had already started. Betty told the lady that was okay, walked into the theater and took a seat near the back. Then came the tears once again. Even though the movie starred Clark Gable, one of Betty's favorite movie stars, she never saw the movie. She saw the screen, but not the movie. Thoughts of Kentucky, her family, Arvin having sex with another woman, bootlegging, the girls, the boys, Dr. Russell, Serena, they all seemed to blend into one mixed up vision in her mind. *"City dreams, city dreams, Arvin and his city dreams."* Her thoughts were interrupted by the lights coming on. The movie had ended. Betty got up and ushered out of the theater with everyone else.

Betty really didn't feel much better. However, she felt more clear minded. She would talk to Arvin and get his side of the story. She was sure there was an explanation. Maybe she hasn't worked hard enough or maybe she's been too naggy. Oh, she didn't know what to think. All of a sudden, she heard what sounded like gun shots. She had heard that noise before with all the crime that had been running rampant in the city. These shots sounded different. They were closer.

Unbeknownst to Betty, she had been sitting in the theater with John Dillinger. The shots she heard were the shots fired between Dillinger and the FBI as he left the theater.

John Herbert Dillinger was an American gangster during the depression era. He ran with a group of men known as the Dillinger Gang or Terror Gang which was accused of robbing 24 banks and four police stations. He was charged with the murder of a police officer in East Chicago. Dillinger had escaped from jail, twice. He evaded the police in four states for almost a year, but returned to Chicago in July, 1934 and met his end at the hand of the police and federal agents. They were informed of his whereabouts by the owner of a brothel where Dillinger had sought refuge at times.

On the night that Betty was sorting out her life, July 22, 1934, the police and several Federal agents moved to arrest Dillinger as he exited the theater. He reached into his vest pocket, but could not draw out his gun then attempted to flee. He was shot four times and killed. Other accounts stated Dillinger ignored a command to surrender, whipped out his gun, then headed for the alley. Federal Agents already had the alley closed off, but Dillinger was determined to shoot it out.

Betty's feet moved her along a bit faster once she heard the shots. She decided to hop onto a streetcar instead of walking all the way back home. She completely forgot about what she had been sad about, and now was concerned about the city being overrun by bad guys shooting guns. Everyone was sleeping by the time she got home. Betty decided to have a cup of tea and calm herself down before she slipped into bed beside her husband. The husband who had cheated on her. The husband who has been lying to her. The husband who had city dreams.

The next morning went just like every other morning. Ruth and Carol left for school, Arvin left for his fake short hours job at the factory, and Betty left to take care of the boys. There was no conversation between Betty and Arvin.

As Arvin was on the way to his brothel, he thought to himself, *Betty knows. Carol told her.* Well, he was glad in a way so he no longer had to keep up the loving husband charade. Although, the loving part had been missing for a long time. Now, he must make a decision. He was wondering what was in Betty's mind.

On the way to her job she felt tired, emotionally tired. Betty knew she needed to stay focused watching three little ones. So, she decided to put her thoughts away and put one foot in front of the other. By the time she reached the home of the boys, her mind was still full of thoughts of the day and night before. She just wanted to get through this day somehow without crying.

Betty was greeted by Mrs. Altman, "Good morning, Betty. The boys already had their breakfast and are ready for their day with you. They sure have taken to you. The talk around our dinner table was all about the lions and tigers at the zoo. Be prepared for them trying to convince you to take them there again today."

Betty responded, "I don't mind. I kinda like the zoo myself. They're good boys."

"Betty, did you see the newspaper this morning?" Mrs. Altman asked.

"No, I usually read yours after you leave. Why?"

"The headline is disturbing. It is "Kill Dillinger Here." The whole first page is about this gangster, John Dillinger, and how he was shot and killed near the Biograph Theater. I'll leave the paper on the table when I leave so you can read it sometime today. What is our city coming to?"

"I don't know. Just so much crime. It is worrisome."

Betty couldn't believe what she just heard. Had she really been in the theater at the same time as that gangster? While she was sitting in the theater having thoughts of a possible ending of her marriage and life as she knew it, Dillinger's life was about to end, period.

Betty went about her day in a fog. She took the boys to the park, pushing each one on the swings, watched them go up a down on the slide, and afterwards took them for ice cream. The whole day felt like she was in a movie in which she was one of the stars, but not playing her part very well. She also didn't like the story line. Her mind went from *Arvin and his city dreams to what could I have done different or better.* Betty kept questioning herself. Her mind started to visualize Arvin and some woman in their bed. She started to feel queasy, sick. Then the tears came once again. She managed to get through the day, but was anxious to get home and talk to Arvin. As she started to climb the stairs to their apartment, she wondered what Arvin would say. Well, she didn't have to wait too long now since she was home.

As soon as Betty got home, she said, "Ruth, take Carol down to the drugstore for a soft drink, I want to talk to your pa when he gets home, which should be any second."

"Aw, momma, do I have to?" Ruth complained.

"Yes. I don't want you girls around this evening," Betty answered.

"Alright," Ruth said reluctantly.

Ruth begrudgingly left and took Carol. As they were leaving, they met Arvin coming in. Neither girl acknowledged him.

"Glad you're home Arvin. I wanna talk to you," Betty said as soon as Arvin walked through the door.

"Betty, you mean you want to nag at me, don't ya?!" Arvin responded.

"Arvin!" Betty said harshly.

"I know what you want to talk to me about. It's about what Carol told ya. Well, it's true. I'm sorry."

"Why, Arvin? Haven't I been a good wife? Haven't I gone along with you all these years with your city dreams?" Tears started to well up in her eyes as she was speaking. A tear found its way out and rolled down onto her blouse.

"Yes, but that's your job. The truth is, I've been bored since we stopped bootlegging. Maybe even before. Durin' that time I met lots of interestin' people, different kinds of people. Lots of things to talk about. You never have anything interestin' to say. You nag me about everything. You're not interested in sex no more. In short, you're boring."

Betty tried to contain herself, but the tears started to flow, until she just started sobbing. She didn't know what to think. She didn't know what to say. She just stood there.

"Stop cryin' and say something," Arvin demanded.

Betty couldn't stop sobbing. She tried to speak in between sobs. But her words came out all choppy. "H...how cou...could you? How l...ong have you b...een with this woman?"

"Not important. What's important is I don't want to be with you no more. Let's figure this out. Let's talk about what's best for the girls?" Arvin quickly responded.

"Don't you mean, what's best for you? Arvin, you don't care about the girls, you never have. You don't even know them. Your city dreams have destroyed us, our family," Betty answered sarcastically.

"Maybe so, but the fact remains, I need to move on from you. It's probably best that I leave tonight. We can talk tomorrow and can work out the details of our divorce."

"Divorce? Details? What details?" Betty gasped. Betty was starting to feel herself getting angry and said, "On what grounds will you divorce me? You are the one that committed adultery."

"You're right. But, you will divorce me and you will give me my freedom," Arvin said emphatically.

...and that is what happened. Betty gave Arvin the divorce. She was tired of the arguing and felt somewhat threatened by Arvin. He had changed so much that she really didn't know what he was capable of doing. He had so many cop friends and didn't want to put her girls or herself in any kind of danger. Betty and the girls moved on and Arvin moved in with Lori.

CHAPTER 20

Changes Ain't Easy

Betty's life changed and so did Carol's. Betty got Carol settled in a boarding school in Momence, Illinois. Although Betty was not a practicing Catholic, the church had arranged it and was taking care of the tuition. She was trying to get her life in order. Ruth moved in with a girlfriend close to where she worked, and Betty found a studio apartment in her building. Everyone was getting settled into their new routine, in a life none of them had planned. Betty continued watching the three boys during the week and on the weekends, she cleaned people's houses. She didn't have time to think about how her life had changed in one afternoon. It had been several months since the divorce and Carol had been in the boarding school most of that time. She called Betty every week and the conversation, for the most part, was the same.

"Momma, I don't like it here," Carol would say.

"Hush Carol, it's what has to be done. Just for a little longer until I can get better settled," Betty would answer.

Today, the conversation went pretty much the same way. However, Carol pushed a little harder this day saying, "But momma. I'm old enough to take care of myself. I'm twelve years old, not a baby."

"Stop!" Betty said harshly. Then she realized that she was just tired and shouldn't have taken it out on Carol. So, she added, "I'm sorry. Serena and I will visit you tomorrow. I'll make my fried chicken that you like and we can have a picnic when we get there. Would you like that?"

"I guess so. I'd rather go home. Momma, I miss you. I miss our home," Carol responded.

"I miss you, too. But with your dad gone things are different now. I'm not home much anymore."

"Is Ruth still living with her girlfriend? I could live with them."

"Now Carol, Ruth is 20 years old, has got herself a nice job. She is busy with her job and her boyfriend. I'll see you tomorrow."

∂◦◦

That year, 1934, was arguably one of the worst years of the Great Depression as the world's economy hit rock bottom. During this period there were people who were jumping out of windows because they lost everything they had and then there were people capitalizing on this financial depression and creating their fortune.

∂◦◦

Arvin was somewhere in between. Arvin and Lori were living together at his brothel. His girls were busier than ever. He had saved money from the bootlegging. Although, he and Betty did live on some of it when he lost his job. As part of the divorce Betty and Arvin split the rest of the savings. There was still a considerable financial stash that Betty was not aware of. With that stash and the eggs he was collecting from his hens, he was sitting pretty.

It appeared that while some people stood in food lines, others were frequenting bars and seeing their favorite prostitute. Since

Arvin's girls did not work the streets, like so many of their counterparts, they commanded a higher fee for their discretion. Arvin still dealt with a lot of the higher city officials and had a lot of the cops in his back pocket. He did, however, have to deal with some of the mob's runners who demanded their percentage, but did manage to make a deal with them as well. He ran numbers from the brothel for the mob and actually got a percentage from them. Arvin had become a smooth wheeler and dealer. He was living his city dreams.

⚬⚬⚬

The family that Betty worked for gave her a week off. They knew she had been through a lot. Betty was working weekends in addition to watching the boys. In fact, they paid her for her time off, something that was unheard of for domestic help. The first day Betty had off, she called Serena to see if she could come by. Serena agreed and they spent the afternoon in one of their long chats.

As they were sipping their tea and enjoying the pastries that Serena usually brought, Serena asked with concern, "Betty, how you doing since Arvin and you split?"

"Aw, he was no good. I'm better off without him," Betty quickly answered.

"I'm so sorry Betty. Things will get better."

"Ruth blames me for him leavin' and I sure do miss Carol. Momence is over 50 miles away and takes so long to get there. Arvin does pick her up every now and then and brings her by for a couple of minutes. But I'm usually workin' and sometimes don't even get to see her," Betty said with tears in her eyes.

"Betty, you just have to stop working so much and have some fun. I have an idea. Go with me tonight, would you?"

"Where to?"

"You know I go to all the democratic meetings downtown. There's some kind of new legislation that is going to be proposed. Oh, come with me. There's lots of nice people there."

"Well, okay, since I don't have to watch the boys tomorrow. They sure do wear me out. It'll be nice to go somewhere different for a change. It seems all I do is watch the boys and clean wealthy peoples' houses. I don't even go to the store all that often anymore. However, I am grateful for the time the family gave me off."

"Well, grab a wrap and let's go. We can stop by my apartment on the way so I can grab mine. I'm so glad you had off so we could get together."

"Me too. Glad you're not livin' out in Northbrook anymore. I'm happy to see you more often."

CHAPTER 21

John

Serena and Betty stayed friends all throughout each other's ups and downs. Serena loved Betty and knew way before Betty found out that Arvin was, as Betty put it, "No good." Arvin had tried to get her to go out with him. At first, she thought it was a harmless gesture, however, when he put his arm around her and whispered in her ear something to the effect that he would like to bed her, she realized what he really wanted. She never told Betty.

Serena and Betty continued chatting on the trolley all the way to the meeting.

Serena stood up and said, "Betty, this is our stop. It has been so good to hear you laugh. It's been a long time since you have. Let's go and have some fun"

"Thanks. You're right," Betty said smiling.

"Come on, follow me and let's go in." Serena said, waving her hand in the direction of the meeting. Betty followed Serena, feeling a bit nervous, but excited at the same time. They both walked through the door and entered a big room.

They were greeted by a nice looking man that said, "Welcome ladies. Glad you came." Then he turned to Serena and asked,

"Who's your friend?"

Serena quickly answered, "John, this is Betty Jamison, a longtime friend."

"Nice to meet you Mrs. Jamison," John said.

"It's Betty and nice to meet you as well," Betty said.

"Well, Betty, come on in and get yourself something to eat. Can I get you ladies something to drink?" John asked.

"Some coffee would be nice," Serena answered.

I'll take some, too. Thank you," Betty said on the heels of Serena's request.

John and Betty talked all evening. He even told Serena that he would take Betty home. He was smitten. That meeting was the beginning of John and Betty's courtship. Betty was happy for the first time in such a long time. She didn't care that he was almost twenty years older than she. They enjoyed each other's company and it didn't hurt that she was a democrat for he was an alderman for one of the districts.

❧❧

Each district in Chicago is represented by an alderman who is elected by their constituency to serve a four-year term. In addition to representing the interests of their ward residents, the fifty aldermen comprise the Chicago City Council.

❧❧

John took Betty to every one of his meetings. She really didn't understand all this talk about new legislation, but she did enjoy being with John. It was nice after watching the boys, to come home get dressed up, and go out.

After courting for a year, John asked Betty to marry him, and of course, Betty said yes. One night when John and Betty were having dinner, the discussion turned to their wedding.

"Betty, do you mind if we get married in city hall?" John asked.

Without hesitation Betty answered, "No, John, I don't mind. Since my divorce situation doesn't allow us to get married in the church, getting married at city hall seems to be the best thing to do."

"Let's get married next weekend. What do you say?" John asked anxiously.

"I would like my daughter Carol to be part of it, as well as Ruth. Carol is fifty miles from here, in that boarding school I told you about. It will take some doing to get her here."

"Let's get her here for the wedding and have her stay. She can live with us. You know I have a big house. You gave your notice to the Altman's, didn't you?"

"Yes, today was my last day. I also told the agency that I wouldn't be cleaning on the weekends any more either," Betty said smiling.

"Good. So, it's settled then. We can drive down in my car and pick up Carol and let the nuns know she's not coming back," John said emphatically.

"I'd better call them and let them know," Betty said happily.

It had been two years since Betty and Arvin's divorce. Arvin had gotten himself one of those snazzy automobiles, as he put it. He picked up Carol twice a month and brought her to the brothel and she stayed with him and Lori. His ladies entertained Carol by doing her hair and putting make-up on her. Carol loved hanging out with these pretty ladies. She never really knew what they did for a living nor knew that they worked for her dad. She missed her mom terribly and didn't really understand why her dad didn't bring her to see momma.

Carol did appreciate the once a month visit with her mom. Betty would take the train and then the bus the fifty plus miles to spend the day with her. It was all she could manage to do since she was working most of the time. The train ride gave her the much needed alone time. Sometimes she just let the tears flow.

Round and round her mind went. She would get lost in her thoughts. *What happened? Where did things go wrong? What did she do wrong? Why did Arvin need another woman? Who was she? How did he meet her? Did he meet her at the factory? I failed at my marriage. I failed as a wife. I failed as a mother. Ruth doesn't like me. I had to send Carol away. The only thing I seem to be good at is cleaning other peoples' houses or watching other peoples' children...and oh yes, bootlegging for her husband.*

Betty usually beat herself up on each train ride. The last ride had been different. Her mind was filled with John. Her mind wandered back to the night they met. She had been feeling really low that night. Serena had invited her out and would not take no for an answer. What a grand night. She met people who seemed interested in her...and of course she met John. That train ride had been her happiest.

Betty was so excited to call Carol and give her the good news that she could hardly dial the number. When Carol got to the phone, Betty excitedly said, "Hi Carol, it's momma."

"Hi momma, is everything okay?" Carol said concerned.

"Everything is just fine," Betty quickly answered.

"When Sister Mary Ellen told me I had a phone call, I got scared something was wrong. Momma, why did you call?" Carol asked.

"There's a lot to tell you. John asked me to marry him and he wants you to live with us," Betty said.

"Oh momma, that makes me so happy! When?" Carol shrieked with joy.

"He wants us to drive down this weekend to pick you up so we can get married next weekend. Is that okay with you?"

Carol answered almost before Betty could get her last word out, "Of course. Yes, yes, yes. Perfect time. We just finished a semester. Would I go to school in the city?"

"Yes, and I think you are ready for high school."

"Oh, momma, I can't wait until you get here. I'm gonna go pack now," Carol said almost forgetting to say goodbye.

"See you in a couple of days. Good bye."

"Bye momma. I love you," Carol said with tears of joy in her eyes.

Carol started jumping up and down with excitement. She started pulling out her clothes from the drawers, folding them and putting them in piles. Sometimes, she folded the same clothes over again. She was so excited.

Betty felt good. Her heart felt the warmth of Carol's words, "I love you momma." She was excited about having Carol with her again. Of course, she was also excited about getting married. She couldn't wait to tell John that she talked with Carol.

As soon as John came to pick her up, she said, "John, it's all set. I called the school and talked to Carol. She is so excited about coming to live with us."

"Good", John said, then continued, "Betty, you have to make one more call."

"Who do I have to call?

"Your landlord. I know you have to give them a two weeks' notice, but you can move in with me next week. After all, we will be married by then."

"You're right. Oh my! Okay. Can I bring some of my things?" Betty asked.

"Whatever you want to bring is fine." John answered.

CHAPTER 22

Take Off My Nightgown

Betty and John picked up Carol and met Ruth and her boyfriend at city hall. Serena was Betty's witness and John's brother Harry was his. They all gathered in the courtroom where John and Betty got married by the judge and when the gavel came down pronouncing that John and Betty were now husband and wife, tears could be seen in Carol and Serena's eyes. Betty was glowing and John seemed so proud.

They all left city hall and everyone headed for a small gathering at John's house, Betty's new home. Betty had never been in the house. John always picked her up and their whole courtship was spent between eating some of Betty's fine home cooking and a neighborhood diner. They spent many an evening at the movies, the Biograph Theater or just taking a ride on the weekends.

Betty was shocked to see the enormity of her new home. She knew John's house was a three- story brick single family residence. However, she would never have guessed the house was 5,500 square feet. It had five bedrooms, six bathrooms, country size kitchen, and formal dining room with an oak plate rack that runs around the room three quarters up the walls, a parlor with oak window seats as well as beautiful oak floors all throughout the house.

The mood of the house was wonderfully festive. As the evening wound down coming to an end John and Betty said their farewells to their family and friends and were ready to settle in for the night. They were both anxious to be alone.

Betty was about to ask which room was Carol's when she heard John say, "Carol you can sleep in the parlor, it has a sunroom which will be perfect for you. I'll have your mom make up the divan for you. All your things are upstairs in your mom's and my room. We can bring those downstairs tomorrow."

"John, we never talked about Carol sleeping in the parlor. I just thought she would take one of the rooms upstairs," Betty said surprised.

"Betty, all the upstairs rooms are rented out, with the exception of ours," John answered sheepishly.

"Rented out? I didn't know?" Betty responded.

"I'm sorry Betty. I just never thought about it. Although, that really isn't the truth. I didn't tell you because I was afraid you wouldn't want to share my home with me. Since I lived alone in such a big house, I rented out four of the bedrooms. You know that my dad left my brother and I this house. Harry already had his own house and family. I was stuck with this huge place. So, I rented out some four of the rooms. It's sort of a boarding house," John explained.

"John, it's okay. It is a big place. I wouldn't want to live here alone either. Let me get Carol bedded down and let's get to bed ourselves. It has been a long day," Betty responded.

"Good night Carol," Betty said and then added, "I'm sorry, I didn't know."

"Good night momma. I don't mind sleeping in the parlor. The sunroom is like my own little sanctuary and sure is better than the dorm at school," Carol said.

Betty and John retired to their room after getting Carol settled. Betty just gasped when she saw their bed. It was so big. There were four beautiful tall maple hand carved posters at each corner of the bed, two maple dressers sitting side by side, and a maple dressing table with a three-sided mirror.

"Oh, John. This room is beautiful!" Betty exclaimed.

"I'm glad you like it. All this was my mother's. When you said you would marry me, I had it all set up in this room for you, for us. Tomorrow you can get all settled in, but for now, let's get some sleep. It has been a long day."

Betty's new life was so far removed from her small farm in Kentucky or the settlement house where she and Arvin had started their new life together in Chicago. Their first apartment would have fit completely in her new dining and parlor room. John was one of those high city officials that she and Arvin use to bootleg for. Betty never had her own city dream. If she had, she knew it would look like this.

Carol started to attend a local high school and settled into the parlor's sunroom as her space in the house. At times, she was uncomfortable sleeping in the open room when the men boarders would come downstairs and pass through to the kitchen or to leave the house. She kept that to herself not to stress out her mom.

After a short while, John expected Betty to clean the house and provide meals for his boarders. Betty was used to hard work, so she didn't mind. She felt it was a trade-off for the life she had been given to her and Carol.

Ruth didn't approve of her marriage. She felt all John wanted was a housekeeper and reminded Betty of that every time they got together. Serena saw it the same way. After a while, Betty began to see it that way, as well. She started keeping to herself more reflecting on her life.

Late one afternoon, Carol came into the kitchen where Betty was preparing food for the house. Betty was surprised by what she saw and said, "Carol, where did you learn to put all that stuff on your face?"

"The ladies that live in pa's building," Carol responded.

"What do you mean the ladies that live in pa's building?" Betty questioned.

"Papa lives upstairs of some ladies who would watch me when he had to leave. They would do my hair and show me how to put make-up on. They were very beautiful and had really pretty clothes."

"Well, take that stuff off your face. You're not going out like that," Betty said firmly.

"But momma, it's the dance at school. It's my first dance. Can I wear the lipstick?"

"Wash your face and will talk about the lipstick."

Carol went into the bathroom and washed off all the makeup, then put on a little lipstick and went back into the kitchen for her mom's approval.

"How's this? I just put on a light pink lipstick," said Carol.

"That's fine. Remember, don't be messing around with them boys," Betty said.

"Momma!" Carol responded slightly embarrassed. Then she kissed her mom on the cheek and said, "Bye, I love you."

"Good bye. Remember, be good now and stay away from them boys," Betty said as Carol was leaving the house.

❦

As the years rolled by, John and Betty's marriage stayed pretty much the same. Betty would spend her days preparing and cooking meals for their boarders and cleaning up after everyone. John went to work and still attended his political meetings. Serena and Betty would have their weekly tea. Betty was content, not really happy, but content. She had a home, a husband, and a good friend.

❦

World War II, also known as the Second World War, was a global war that lasted from 1939 to 1945. The Empire of Japan aimed to dominate Asia and the Pacific and in 1937 was already at war with the Republic of China. But the world war is generally said to have begun on September 1, 1939 with the invasion of Poland by Nazi Germany. France and the United Kingdom entered the war shortly afterwards.

Time marched on. Ruth got married, got pregnant, and had a little boy. Her husband got drafted into the war. Ruth's husband was sent to Germany and ultimately was killed at the battle over the bridge at Remagan. Carol met a young man, fell in love, quit school, and got married. She told her friends that one of the reasons she got married was to get out of the house. Sleeping in the parlor's sunroom with men boarders walking around was becoming very, very uncomfortable for her. Her new husband's family found them a house to rent on the south side near them. Shortly thereafter they had a baby girl.

One night, she came home after being out with her mom, Betty, and walked in on a very surprised husband. He was not only entertaining another woman, but this woman was wearing her nightgown. She flew into a rage, called a friend, packed a suitcase, grabbed her daughter, and left. That was the end of that marriage.

The great depression was over. While the city was recuperating from the many losses caused by the depression, the country entered the war with Japan. Japan had attacked Pearl Harbor, Hawaii, causing the deaths of 2,403 Americans and wounded another 1,178. The 32nd president of the United States, Franklin Delano Roosevelt, died the same year the war ended.

Arvin's prostitute business started to fail due to the girls going out on their own. As time went on, prostitution was moving to the suburbs. Lori ran off with one of her old clients. Jobs once again became available in the garment factories and Arvin went back to work. After several years on the job, he caught his hand in one of the milling machines and lost several of his fingers. He ended up in the hospital, fell in love with his attending nurse, and got married. Lori ran off with one of her old clients.

CHAPTER 23

Farewell

One afternoon when Betty was preparing food for the house's dinner, she heard a knock at the door. When she answered and opened it, she was quite surprised to see John's brother standing on the other side of it.

Before she could say anything, Harry said, "Betty, John has been taken to the hospital."

"What happened Harry?" Betty quickly asked.

Harry answered as he entered the house, "He collapsed at the meeting. Come on, let me take you there."

Betty grabbed her purse and keys and asked, "Oh, Harry, what do you think is wrong?"

"Betty, I think my brother had a heart attack," Harry answered.

Betty started crying and muttering over and over, "I hope not, I hope not, I hope not."

Harry continued to console Betty on the way to the hospital, although, he feared the worse.

Harry and Betty approached the window of the emergency room and Harry said, "We are here to see John Payson. This is his wife, Mrs. Payson."

The nurse behind the window said, "Wait here. I'll get his doctor."

It wasn't long before a man with a stethoscope draped around his neck came through a door. As he walked over to them, he asked, "Mrs. Payson?"

"Yes," Betty answered, then asked, "How is my husband?"

"I am so sorry, Mrs. Payson. Your husband had a massive heart attack. We were not able to save him," the doctor said as he escorted Betty to a chair.

"Oh, Harry, what am I going to do without Pa?" Betty said, using the nickname she called him.

Harry sat down next to her, took her hand and said, "Betty, it's going to be okay. Let me take you home. I can take care of the details for my brother's funeral."

Betty then stood up and said, "I want to see him. Doctor, can I see him?"

"Of course. I'll take you both," the doctor replied.

Betty stared down at the lifeless body of her husband of ten years. She had so many thoughts running through her mind that she wasn't able to define what she was really feeling.

Betty turned around and asked, "Harry, will you take me home now?"

"Of course, and Judy and I will stay with you tonight," Harry responded.

"Thanks. I'll call Ruth and Carol and let them know."

Betty was devastated. After she called the girls, she called Serena and asked her if she would come over. Of course, Serena said yes.

When she got off the phone with Serena Betty said, "Harry, you and Judy don't have to stay tonight. Serena is going to stay with me. Please take care of everything for me. I really don't know how to do such things."

"Of course. I'll wait here until your friend gets here," Harry responded.

"No need, she will be here any minute now," Betty said. The truth of the matter was Betty felt she needed a few minutes alone.

Harry reluctantly left Betty. He didn't like leaving her alone in that big house. As he drove away, he saw Serena walking up to the house. He felt relieved.

As soon as Serena walked in the door, she hugged Betty and said, "Betty, I'm so sorry."

"Thanks for coming over. I don't know what I'm going to do without Pa. He took care of everything. This is his house. I don't know what's going to happen to me," Betty said with a worried look on her face.

"Don't go worrying yourself about that now. Let me make you some tea. I'm sure everything will work out," Serena said.

Serena stayed with Betty for the next few days and kept Betty from worrying about what's next.

John's brother, Harry, did make all the arrangements for the funeral. Betty, Ruth, and Carol were in the car that lead over twenty cars meandering through the city heading toward the cemetery. Once all the cars parked, there were city officials, democratic committee heads, district aldermen, family and friends all huddled together around the gravesite. John was an architectural engineer for the city. He was part of the design team for the first expressway in Chicago, but died before he saw it open. His entire team was there from the city, paying tribute to John.

On the way home Carol leaned over and asked, "Momma, how are you doing?"

"I'm fine Carol. Just tired is all. Harry invited some people back to the house, so I'm glad we are on our way home," Betty responded.

When Betty got home, there was a sea of people. People coming in with pies, cakes, sandwiches, casseroles, and food of all kinds. She wasn't up to being with so many people. Betty paid her respects to everyone, went upstairs and passed out on the bed that she once shared with her husband. Carol curled up next to her. They both slept through the night.

CHAPTER 24

A Million Years Ago

As the weeks went by, Betty was trying to figure out what she was going to do. Harry informed Betty that she could no longer stay in the house. Since Betty didn't have a job, or money of her own, she packed up her things, which primarily consisted of clothing, a few knick-knacks, and a doll her mother had given her and moved in with Carol and her new husband, Richard.

Richard was at a military base in Georgia, training troops for the Korean War. Carol and her daughter, Ann, were about to leave and join him. Carol lived in the downstairs of a two flat, like the one Arvin had when he was in the business of prostitution. Carol's sister, Ruth lived upstairs with her son. Carol suggested Betty stay in their place while they were gone. Betty agreed, since she really didn't have any means of getting her own place.

Carol and Ann, left for Georgia and Betty settled herself in and invited Serena over for the first day Serena had off. When Betty saw Serena walking up the stairs, she quickly opened the door and said,

"Serena, thank you for coming over. I've been so down since I lost Pa. Carol and Richard are in Georgia so I can stay here for a while. Ruth is upstairs with my grandson, Danny. You know she and I don't get along very well. It's been like that since before Arvin and I split. After the divorce, things just got worse She's just an angry girl."

"I'm sorry Betty," Serena said. "Arvin didn't know how blessed he was. I remember when I first met you. Remember? You looked so scared and lost in that settlement house. We went to that agency to get you a job and had pastries afterwards. Remember?" Serena asked.

Betty answered with a smile on her face, "Yes. That feels like a million years ago. So much has happened since then. When Arvin and I left Kentucky, I thought we would love and support each other forever."

"Well, you certainly loved and supported him. When you started bootlegging for him I thought that was putting you in real danger. You had so many people coming in and out of your place. I was glad when your home brewing business moved down into the basement. At least no more people had to go into your place to get their drink."

"Yes, that was scary at times. Arvin not being home, and there I was filling jugs for men. I used to do that for my brothers back home, but we didn't have to bother with gangsters," Betty said.

"You did good by Arvin. He done you wrong. You worked like a dog for him. I was so happy when you met John and you guys got married. You deserved a good life. But every time I came over you were cleaning something or cooking for those boarders," Serena said. She added with anger in her voice, "It is against everything that is good for his brother to ask you to leave."

"Serena, oh, maybe the only good I can do in this life is to be someone's wife and help them with their city dreams. I'm not much good for anything else," Betty said with resignation in her tone.

"Hush! That's what you always say when someone talks foolishness," Serena said quickly.

"It seems that the only reason John married me was to be his housekeeper and his cook."

"Oh Betty, it's time for the "hush" again. I'm sure that John loved you. You know that these men just don't know how to show you, let alone say it," Serena said, then asked, "Did you feel loved?"

"No, not really. He let Carol stay with us. However, he made her sleep in the parlor. Even though it had a sunroom, it was still pretty much open. When she left that no good first husband of hers, John wouldn't let her come to the house with the baby. That wasn't right. It wasn't her fault that she had to leave him. After all, she walked in on him and another woman and the worse part was the woman was wearing Carol's nightgown."

"Well, one thing is for sure, Betty. You are a first-class best kind of friend," Serena said, then got up and hugged her.

"Thanks. However, I feel like you have been a better friend to me than I have been to you. Serena, I just don't know what I'm going to do. I can stay here for a while, but I am going to have to get a job to make ends meet."

"Did John leave you any money?"

"No. However, Harry has all the paperwork and I might be able to get part of his pension from the city. That will take a while though. Someone told me that the zoo is looking for cleaning people. I certainly have a lot of experience in that area. I might take the bus this week and find out what they are looking for," Betty said.

"Betty, I'm sorry you have to do such hard work," Serena responded.

"That's okay. I think that's the only thing I'm good at. Cleaning and cooking," Betty answered with a tone of resignation in her voice.

"Okay, here comes another "hush" with that kind of talk. You just haven't had the time to find out what you would like to do. You've been so busy doing things for other people."

"Maybe you're right. Maybe someday I will do something important like Arvin and John."

"What did Arvin do that was important?!" Serena exclaimed.

"He built a home brewing business and that was important to

some cops, and some city officials."

"That wasn't important, that was illegal and he dragged you into that. Betty, don't give him so much credit. I'm sorry, I know you loved him, but he used you to get his city dreams, whatever that means...and then he left you. Not a nice man." Serena looked at the time and said, "Well, it's late. I'd better get home and let you get some sleep."

"That you so much for coming over. I feel better. Be careful going home. Good bye." Betty said as she hugged her friend.

CHAPTER 25

Bushman

Betty did take that bus to the Lincoln Park Zoo, and was offered a job as part of a cleaning crew. She helped clean out the public bathrooms, exhibit halls and animal cages. It was a hard, dirty job, but Betty did it without complaint. She was grateful to be able to save the money she was making. Carol and her husband had been gone about a month, and sent word they would be gone about a year. Living at their place was giving her renewed hope in the future.

Betty was lost in her thoughts, cleaning out one of the cages, when she felt something behind her. It was a gorilla. She screamed and hurled her mop toward the animal. Next thing she felt was a pinch on her buttocks from the gorilla's fingers. If that had been a man, she would have slapped him.

From nowhere came a loud voice, "Bushman, no! Bushman, come!"

Bushman came to the Lincoln Park Zoo in 1930. He had been

orphaned as an infant in Cameroon in West Africa and was sold to the zoo for $3,500 by a Presbyterian missionary and an animal trader. He appeared in newsreels and became an international attraction. He was photographed often, and was a temperamental subject, often hurling food and his dung at photographers.

But no other animal in a Chicago-area zoo had ever drawn the crowds like Bushman did in his stark, steel cage. People came from all over to see him. One day someone threw a pair of sunglasses in his cage and Bushman put them on. From that day forward people gave Bushman everything from cigars, which he did put in his mouth, to all kinds of food. Once a week his trainer would bring him out on the lawn and together they would perform simple tricks for the crowd. The trainer would wrestle with Bushman to the squeals and the delight of the children. Since Bushman weighed 550 lbs., some worried about the trainer putting his life in danger. However, the two seemed to have a mutual respect for each other.

∽∾

The booming loud voice came again, "Bushman, come!" Bushman was not listening to his trainer. Eventually Bushman left Betty alone. He scurried down the hallway of the exhibit hall, into the kitchen, and back into the corridor, where his cage was housed. Bushman had roamed around for nearly three hours until a harmless garter snake frightened him back into his cage.

A tall, brawny man approached Betty and asked, "Are you alright?"

Betty answered faintly, "I think so." Then asked, "Who are you?"

"I'm Busman's trainer and handler," the man answered.

"He scared the daylights out of me. He pinched my bottom."

"Sorry. I don't know where he picked that up. He has pinched my behind a couple of times, too. You know how he mimics people. He must have seen someone do this. Glad you're alright."

"Thanks. No one will believe that a gorilla pinched my behind."

"Tell them to come talk to me and I'll tell them that it's true...I saw it!" The handler said with a chuckle.

Bushman died on New Year's Day in 1951. For the next several weeks, mourners filed past his cage. His mounted remains are displayed at the Field Museum of Natural History for all to see. Betty's job at the zoo came to an end. She continued to take different domestic jobs to include passing out towels in bathrooms, or powder rooms, at fancy hotels and cleaning the offices of city hall in downtown Chicago.

Ruth decided she wanted to sell the two flat. It was becoming a financial struggle for her since Carol and Richard weren't able to contribute to the building, like they did in the beginning. Richard was getting military pay and although, he did not lose his job, there was no income from it. She discussed this with Richard and Carol and they agreed. So, Ruth did sell it and handled all the details of the sale. She and her son, Danny, moved into a home with her in-laws. Betty was again, literally homeless. Ruth found her a one room flat in a rooming house in the city.

Richard was transferred to a California military base and knew that when they came back to Chicago, they also would be literally homeless.

As usual when things changed in Betty's life, she called Serena. She told Serena that she moved and was now living in a rooming house in the city. Serena decided to call on Betty to cheer her up. When Betty heard the knock at the door, she was so excited for she knew it was Serena.

As soon as the door opened, Serena said, "Betty, I can't believe you had to move again. Well, here, I brought us some pastries so put on some coffee and let's talk.

As Betty was putting on the coffee, she said, "It's not so bad. I like having my own space. This is the first time in my life that I do. There is just a small kitchen, but it has everything I need to cook for myself. I also have a pull-down bed. I don't even mind sharing a bathroom with people, and it's right down the hall."

"I'm glad that you're not sad about all this. I kind of like this little place. It's cozy," Serena said with a smile.

"Yes, and not so much to clean. I also like facing a busy street. Sitting in front of the window, having my tea, and watching the cars go by feels nice. Not so sure why. Maybe it's because in the past this would have been considered foolish idle time."

Betty, I am glad you have some time to enjoy your life."

"Yes, I actually have been enjoying my granddaughter, Ann. Carol and Richard are back. Richard was to be sent to Korea, but the military discharged him due to him being a family man. That would have been a hardship. You know he fought in WWII, so I'm glad he didn't have to go overseas again. They have an apartment on the near north side. Ann spends some weekends with me. I love my time with her."

"How old is she now?"

"She's almost twelve years old."

"Betty, how are you with money?"

"I'm doing alright. I was able to save my money while I was living in Carol and Richard's place. I'm still working at city hall, but my shift is only three nights a week. I'll stay there for a while. Although, when I get home from my shift, I'm achy all over. I am saving as much money as I can because I want to take my granddaughter, Ann, to California for her eighth-grade graduation in a year."

Serena shrieked with joy and said, "Oh Betty that will be so good for both of you. You have never taken any time off from working since I've known you, and how long is that now? About forty some years?"

Betty did save enough money to take Ann to California,

specifically Disneyland. This new amusement park had opened the year before and had become the talk of the nation. Betty had Carol plan the trip while keeping it a surprise from Ann. Graduation day came and so did the card from Betty that included bus tickets to California.

Ann jumped up and hugged Betty as soon as she opened her card, "Oh, Gramma, I love you. Thank you, thank you, thank you!"

They set off for their adventure on a bus, actually several busses, and arrived in California three days later safe and sound. Betty and Ann spent a full day at Disneyland and went on every ride. They ate food in Chinatown, took a cable car up a hill from one street to another, visited a famous cemetery and even visited several parks. It was a grand trip. Ann and Betty had always been bonded. However, this trip really gave them time to get to know each other in a much deeper way.

On the way back to Chicago, they both laid their heads back and reflected on their time together. Betty felt like she really did something wonderful. Something she could never have done for her own children. She felt gratified and fulfilled probably for the first time in her life.

CHAPTER 26

Fire!

Betty returned to her city hall job and things seemed to be going smoothly in her life. She was recouping the money she had spent on the trip to California, and even managing to put a little aside. She still lived in her one room flat, and it became her place of refuge.

One night, while she was at her city hall job, a fire broke out in the building. One of Betty's crew members asked her if she smelled smoke.

"Yes. Do you think someone is smoking?" Betty asked.

"No. Our crew knows not to smoke on the job. I think it is a fire somewhere in the building," her crew member responded.

"Where is everybody?" Betty asked.

"Our crew is all over these top floors. So, we're all pretty close. Let's go into the hall and see what is going on," Betty's co-worker said.

"Smoke! There! It's coming from under that door!" Betty yelled.

"Come on, we'd better get out of here. Let's take the stairs," her crew member said.

Betty and her co-worker opened the door to the stairwell. They could see flames coming from below and some of their crew coming down the stairs. They met in the stairwell and went back into the hallway.

They all seem to say at the same time, "What do we do?"

"Well, we can't go down, that's for sure and I don't want to go back up. I guess we'll just have to wait here," one of the crew said.

"I hear the alarm. Someone must have reported the fire," Betty said.

"Listen, fire engines! The smoke is getting pretty bad," a crew member said.

"Let's get into the other room. Maybe the smoke is not that bad in there," Betty suggested.

Carol and Ruth watched the commotion on television. The announcer reported that the fire was out of hand, raging on the first, second and third floors. It was reported that the cleaning crew was trapped in the upper floors of city hall. They knew their mom was working there that night and were glued to the television. Firemen were hosing the building and all of a sudden, they saw a ladder being raised up to one of the windows.

Betty's co-worker shouted, "Betty, guys, over here. By the window. Firemen are raising a ladder and are helping people out of the window from the floor below."

"Do they see us up here?" Someone asked.

"I think so," Betty responded.

Just then they heard a voice shouting from below through what looked like a megaphone, "We're coming up to get you guys out. Get ready."

Betty and her crew watched the last person being helped down the ladder from the floor below. At the same time the ladder was being elevated up to them, the smoke started to pour into the room. There were four of them that had to be helped out.

A fireman appeared at the window. He asked, "Is everyone here?"

"Yes, just the four of us," one of the crew said.

"Okay, single file. Come on, take my hand and don't look down," the fireman instructed.

Betty was the first to be helped out onto and down the ladder. The remaining three men also made it out successfully. Ruth and Carol let go a sigh of relief when it was announced all thirty people who were in the building were out safely. It was the first of several more fires in that city hall. Betty stopped working for that cleaning crew and took a job at an amusement park collecting tickets. She was done with being a janitress. A gorilla was one thing, but a fire was too much.

☙❧

The years rolled by. Betty took tickets at the amusement park during the summer. She enjoyed visits from Ann, who was older now and married. Betty still lived in her one room flat. She and Ann had many a sleep over in that Murphy bed, but now she usually met Ann for dinner. She was content; not necessarily fulfilled, but content. Serena would come by now and then for their "girl time."

One day, Serena happened to just stop by, which was out of the norm. Usually their visits were planned. So, when she knocked on the door, it surprised Betty. When Betty opened the door and saw Serena, she squealed with delight and hugged her, then said, "Serena, what are you doing here, although I am glad you stopped by." Then asked another question before Serena had a chance to answer the first one, "Did you bring those delicious pastries?"

Serena laughed and said, "Of course. I took a chance on you

being home, because I wanted to tell you something."

"I'm home most of the winter. The amusement park closes in September, so I'm off until next May. I get to claim unemployment during the winter. What is so important that you had to come all the way over here to tell me?"

"Let's talk over tea." Serena answered, for she wanted to take her time telling Betty.

"Okay." Betty said, then continued, "Here's a plate for the pastries."

As Betty was pouring the tea she asked, "Alright now, tell me."

Serena started with, "There is a program for foster grandmothers at the private medical/psychiatric hospital. They are looking for grandmothers to work with the children that don't have relatives of their own. I thought of you right away. You would be perfect for being a foster grandmother." Then she asked, "What do you say?"

"Oh, I don't know. I kind of like just being by myself these days."

"Come on Betty. You have so much to offer a child. Look at you and Ann. You guys are so close."

"I didn't do so good with my own children. Why would they want me? I've only known cleaning and cooking - and oh yes, can't forget about bootlegging."

"Don't sell yourself so short. I think you would be a wonderful foster grandmother." Then Serena said sternly, "Come on, I'm going to take you over there now. They are taking applications and doing interviews today."

"Oh, I can't go now."

Serena answered in her usual forceful way, "Why not? You're not doing anything today. Grab your coat and let's go."

"Serena, I don't want to go because I don't want to be embarrassed. Like I said, I really don't have anything to offer. That would be hard to hear from a stranger."

"Betty! How could you say that? You have so much to offer and I am sorry that you are not in touch with that." Serena said harshly. Then continued, "Maybe, if you did this you would find out what your gifts are. Maybe you would realize you have so much to offer. Now, I am going to ask you again, can I take you over to apply?"

"You always could get me to do things. Yes, I will change and go with you. Maybe you are right, maybe I do have something to offer and just maybe, through this program, I will find out what it is."

CHAPTER 27

Louie

Serena smiled for she knew Betty's gifts were just hidden, due to Betty's low self-esteem. Arvin's controlling issues, and cheating ways certainly attributed to this along with John using her as a house maid. Then of course, John's family putting her out of the house and not even acknowledging her as family, even though she and John were married for many years.

Serena did take Betty over to the hospital. Betty filled out the application and was asked to stay for an interview.

A man walked out of an office and came over to Betty and said, "Mrs. Payson, my name is Mr. Roberts. Thank you for applying to our Foster Grandmother Program. By looking at your application I can see that you have watched a lot of children over the course of these many years."

"Yes sir, and I have two of my own, two girls and two grandchildren, a boy and a girl," Betty responded.

"Why do you want to be part of our program?" Mr. Roberts asked.

"My friend thought I would be able to do some good with one of the children. She has more faith in me than I have in myself. I have the time, so I thought I would give it a try, if you think I am qualified enough," Betty answered.

"Mrs. Payson, to tell you the truth, we really do need help. We have children who have been placed here who, in some cases, have no real family and who have had some severe trauma in their lives. For example, we have one boy, Louie, who hasn't uttered a word in two years. He came to us in that state after his parents were murdered. The authorities believed him to be retarded or mentally ill. However, we don't believe he is mentally ill or retarded. We think he has been traumatized and has himself locked up inside. Louie has had several foster grandmothers. None have been able to get through to the boy. If you're willing to take him on, you can start anytime."

Betty gasped and said, "Oh my, so fast! I didn't think I would be approved so quick. I don't even know if I can do any good."

"Louie needs someone to work with who he can trust. I think your friend is right. I can see something in you that possibly could unlock him. You are soft, yet I can tell you could be firm when necessary. And I think you might just have the kind of heart that we need in our program. I don't want to see Louie get lost in the system. If we can't see some improvement in him soon, that is exactly what will happen. The state will institutionalize him. We don't want to see that happen. Are you willing to try Betty?" Mr. Roberts asked.

Betty felt herself acquiescing, "Yes, I will try. I just hope I can do some good so I don't disappoint you."

Mr. Roberts responded quickly, "Betty, I don't think you could disappoint anyone. No matter how things turn out, I will have known you gave it your all." He then continued, "We would need you every day for a couple of hours, and it is all voluntary. Is that okay with you?"

"Yes, however, I don't drive so I will need to take a bus," Betty said.

"That is not a problem. You will be given tokens for the bus."

Betty and Mr. Roberts continued to work out all the details and when Betty told Serena the conversation on the way home,

Serena just smiled. She knew this was going to change Betty's life.

Betty agreed to try to work with Louie as a foster grandmother. She was a little nervous for this was pushing her out of her comfort zone. She used to just watch children, not work with them in any constructive way. She was too busy cleaning and cooking for them. Also, she was in no position to teach them anything. She actually learned from them. Over the years she did learn to speak more articulately and pronounce the "ings" on her words. She tried to stop joining two words together. However, she still did sometimes.

The next day, Betty took the bus to the hospital, took a deep breath, and walked in. She was greeted by Mr. Roberts, who was standing with a little boy who appeared to be around eight years old.

"Come in Betty. Come meet Louie," Mr. Roberts said. He turned to Louie and continued, "Louie, this is Mrs. Payson. She is going to be spending time with you."

"Nice to meet you, Louie. Would you like to take a walk for a little while?" Betty asked.

Louie nodded.

Betty and Louie walked in silence for a while, then Betty said, "Louie, let's walk over by that bench. We can sit for a while and just enjoy the flowers. They are so pretty. I love flowers, don't you?"

Louie smiled and nodded.

Betty continued, "The flowers that we are looking at are called mums. Sounds like moms, doesn't it?" Louie just listened.

"Mums come in oh so many colors. Most flowers bloom in the spring and summer. Mums are some of the flowers that bloom in the fall. This month is October and is considered the fall. Oh, you probably already knew that. You know, where I was born and grew up, there were lots of trees. I grew up in Kentucky which is a couple of states from here. I lived in a small cabin with my brothers and sisters. Our cabin was surrounded by lots and lots of beautiful red maple trees. All their leaves would turn red and sometimes orange. When I was little, my mom told me that I called them flower trees. Red flower trees. If you look way over there, you can see some of those trees. You can tell by their beautiful red leaves, or as I used to call them, red flower trees. Do you see them?" Betty asked.

Louie nodded his head.

Betty then asked another question, "Louie, am I talking too much?"

Louie shook his head no.

"Do you want me to keep talking?" Betty asked.

Louie smiled.

"Okay then, here comes another question, do you like pancakes?"

Louie smiled.

"Do you put syrup on your pancakes?"

Louie nodded.

Betty went on, "Maple syrup comes from those red maple trees. In the spring my dad would drill a hole in the trunk of the tree and syrup would come out. My mom would heat it up and then do some other things to it. Not sure all what. All I know is that I put it on my pancakes and it was sure good. Louie, my time is up with you. We need to go back inside."

Louie nodded, although he looked a little sad.

Betty took the bus back to her flat, made herself something to eat and just reflected on her time with Louie. She had really enjoyed sitting with Louie and was surprised at how open he was to listening to her. Betty had not thought of her childhood on the farm in Kentucky for so long, that it had felt good to revisit it through the stories she had told Louie. That night she went to bed with a smile on her face for the first time in many years.

The next morning, she got up feeling happier than usual. Betty tried to keep herself busy so she wouldn't keep looking at the clock until it was time to leave to see Louie. She was surprised how she felt toward that little eight-year-old boy. She just met him, yet he had grabbed her heart.

When Betty got off the bus and walked to the hospital, she noticed she had a spring in her step. She felt energized. As soon as she walked through the door, she heard, "Hi Betty. Glad you decided to come back." It was Mr. Roberts. He had been waiting for her.

"I enjoyed sitting with Louie. He is a sweet boy," Betty responded.

"He took a shine to you. This morning he wanted pancakes. Usually we can't get him to eat breakfast. However, this morning he ate all three big pancakes."

"Did he put maple syrup on them?" Betty asked with a smile.

"Yes, he did, why?"

"I told him a story about how my dad use to drill the trunk of our red maples and drain the syrup out," Betty responded.

Mr. Roberts smiled and said, "Betty you made quite an impression on the boy. He is in the day room waiting on you."

Betty smiled back and walked into the day room. She saw Louie sitting by himself and walked over to him and said, "Good afternoon Louie. It's still pretty nice outside would you like to go back to our bench?"

Louie nodded yes.

Betty started her conversation with, "I understand you had pancakes this morning with maple syrup on them."

Louie smiled.

"Did you put butter on them as well?"

Louie nodded yes.

"When I was your age, there weren't stores where we lived. We lived in the hills surrounded by all those maple trees I told you about. So, my mom had to make our butter. Do you want to know how my mom made butter?" Betty asked.

Louie looked up at Betty, smiling and nodded yes.

"Okay then, first of all we had to milk the cows. I hated milking the cows. I would have to sit on these really small stools and half the time I would fall off."

With that, Louis laughed.

Betty continued, "Then once I got settled on this little stool I would grab the udders and pull down on them."

Louie looked up at her with a questioning look.

"That's right, you wouldn't know what an udder was," Betty responded to Louie's questioning look, then continued, "The udders are the long things that hang down from the underside of the cow. I would pull on each udder, which are like fingers, until milk came out. It was hard work. Sometimes the cow would get mad and kick its feet or just plain be stubborn. After I got the milk, mom would let it set for a while and then after a day or so collecting milk she would scoop off the cream. The cream is what settled on top. She would pour the cream in a tall wooden thing and put a stick in it and push it up and down for a long time. The cream finally turned to butter. And it was the best tasting butter ever. So now, every time you put butter on your pancakes, I want you to remember how that butter was made."

Louie had been listening intently and when she stopped talking, he looked like he wanted to say something. But of course, he didn't.

When their session ended that day, Betty felt down. She didn't realize how happy and content she felt telling her stories to Louie until their time ended. She said good-bye to Louie and walked to the bus stop. While waiting for the bus, she reflected on their time together. She also reminisced about her childhood, about her mom, who had passed away some time ago from influenza and the little cabin they lived in. The bus came, Betty stepped up into the bus, took her seat, sat back and just relaxed into her memories until her stop. Again, that night she not only went to bed with a smile, she slept sounder than ever before. She was happy.

Betty met with Louie every day, even though she only had to meet with him during the week. However, she went on the weekends, too. She and Louie had become real close. Each time she came he greeted her with a hug and same when she left. Betty told Louie stories about her life growing up in the hills of Kentucky and about her brothers and sisters. Louie was actually participating in games at the hospital with other children. He laughed and had become more expressive, but still did not speak.

Louie's brother had been placed with a foster family who

wanted to adopt him. However, they weren't willing to take Louie. Betty was given this information and felt if only she could get him to talk, they may change their mind and give Louie a home, too.

She continued to work with him for three more months. It was now midwinter and their special bench was covered with snow most of the time, so they sat in the corner of the day room. Betty would bring hot chocolate in a thermos and homemade cookies.

She came to know the history of the psychiatric/medical facility called Dunning, which was very dark. Betty started to hear stories of the atrocities that had taken place in the years past. Children from poor families placed there to die. Once someone was declared insane they were sent there and locked up. Beds were lined up like army barracks, hygiene was poor, and the food was not sufficient for the number of children there. Everything about Dunning disturbed her and she was determined to see Louie speak. She knew that was his only way out.

CHAPTER 28

Louie and the Brown Puppy Show

One day, Betty asked the administration if it would be possible to take Louie down the street to the local hamburger joint. She did get special permission, which was practically unheard of. But Betty had earned the respect of the administration. Louie was thrilled and couldn't get his jacket on fast enough. Louie and Betty held hands as they walked in the light falling snow. Louie tried to catch the snowflakes on his tongue, but it wasn't snowing hard enough for the snowflakes to stick.

As Betty and Louie walked into the hamburger shop Betty said, "Louie let's each get the hamburger special, what do you say?"

Louie had the biggest smile on his face, which Betty took to mean a great big yes.

Betty ordered two specials and found a table for her and Louie. While they were waiting for their hamburger specials Betty said, "Louie, we have been meeting almost every day now for almost 6 months and I think we trust each other, am I right?"

Louie nodded yes.

"I would like to know why you don't talk. Is it because you can't or don't want to?"

Louie shrugged his shoulders indicating he didn't know.

"If I asked you to try to say a word, would you?"

Louie just shrugged his shoulders again."

Their hamburger specials came and they ate in silence. Betty watched Louie eat and her heart was so happy to see him enjoy his burger and fries, yet, at the same time, her heart was heavy with sadness knowing unless he talked he would be institutionalized. When they finished, Betty asked Louie if he wanted to stop in at the new pet store. And of course, just like any other eight-year-old boy, he nodded his head yes. So, off they went.

As they entered the pet store, Louie seemed overwhelmed with all the activity around him. It became apparent to Betty that Louie had never been in a store like this. Betty suggested that they walk around and see all the different kinds of pets people buy.

Louie's head seemed to spin on his shoulders. He looked at the fish, then the birds, then the kittens. He was all over the store. All of a sudden, his eyes locked onto a small brown puppy that was in the center of the store. It was boxed in by a round fence, but the top was open. Before Betty or anyone knew, Louie reached down and picked up the puppy. He fell backwards and they both crashed to the floor. First Louie, then the puppy. Louie never let go of the puppy and brought himself to a sitting position on the floor. The puppy was wagging its tail and licking all over Louie's face. Louie started to giggle, then rolled backwards trying to hold the puppy away from his face. Betty was smiling along with several customers who were watching the Louie and the Brown Puppy Show. All of a sudden, Betty heard, "I love you."

The only one that seemed startled was Betty. Did she hear what she thought she heard? Did Louie speak? Betty walked over to Louie and said, "Louie, I think it's time to go. Let's put the puppy back now. Maybe we can come back sometime."

Tears welled up in Louie's eyes and he said, "I don't want to go back."

Betty grabbed him and hugged him. "You talked, you said

words," Betty said, then started to cry.

Louie looked up at her and said, "I love you."

"I love you too, Louie," Betty responded.

She did not ask Louie anymore questions. They walked back to the hospital hand in hand through the falling snow. It was coming down harder now and it did stick to Louie's tongue. Betty felt such joy in her heart that she thought it was going to bust open.

She could hardly wait to tell someone at the hospital what just happened. When they walked into the hospital, Mr. Roberts greeted them with, "Welcome back, we were worried about you with the way the snow is now coming down."

Betty shared their experience at the pet store. Mr. Robert's eyes filled with tears as he was listening to Betty. He turned to Louie and asked if he would say something else.

"Of course, what would you like me to say?" Louie asked.

Mr. Robert's just gasped. Then asked, "Why haven't you said anything these past two years?"

"I don't know," Louie said.

Needless to say, there was a lot of activity around this phenomenon. Louie was bombarded by different doctors, all asking him questions. Betty was interviewed by many of the hospital staff, including some of the same doctors. Both Betty and Louie became celebrities at the hospital.

Mr. Roberts suggested that Betty take a week off and rest up, as Louie will be busy with the medical team for testing. So, that is what Betty did. However, she couldn't rest her mind. All she thought about was Louie. She missed him so much. Betty replayed the Louie and puppy show at the pet store over and over in her mind.

Before the week was up, she received a call asking her to come in the next day. Betty became so excited and knew she couldn't spend the day alone. She called Serena and they spent the afternoon together with Betty sharing with her what happened at the pet store.

The next day when Betty got off the bus, she walked a little more deliberately with her head held higher than ever before. She felt good about herself for the first time in her life. As soon as she walked in the door, she was approached by a young man and escorted to the day room. Louie was sitting there with another boy and man and woman. There were cameras and lights all over the room.

Mr. Roberts approached Betty and said, "Betty the news people are here doing a story on you and Louie. They want to ask you a few questions. But first, I want you to know that Louie has undergone testing all week. Louie's cognitive abilities reported within normal range. The foster parents for Louie's brother are here and are considering fostering Louie, as well. All this is happening for Louie because of you. Your love and caring nature provided the safety for Louie to come out of his shell. He has been talking up a storm all week."

Betty was speechless and a bit embarrassed and proud all at the same time.

The evening news reported on Betty Payson and how her loving, caring nature enabled an eight-year-old boy to speak after two years of silence. They interviewed her in depth about the stories she told Louie and about the puppy at the pet store. Louie's background was also reported on, along with the possibility that Louie would be joining his brother and his foster parents.

Betty finally realized she did have something to offer. Even though the news reported how she helped Louie, the truth was, Louie helped her find her joy. Louie helped her find her self-worth. Louie helped her find herself.

The next morning, while she was having her coffee and basking in the joy she felt for herself and Louie, she received a phone call.

"Good morning Betty, I wanted you to know that Louie is going to be leaving us to join his brother," Mr. Roberts said.

"Oh, Mr. Roberts that is wonderful news!" Betty exclaimed.

"Yes, we are all excited about it. Louie asked me to call you to see if you could come by before he leaves," Mr. Roberts said.

"Of course, I'll take the bus right over," Betty replied.

Betty was excited about Louie wanting to see her, yet at the same time felt a little sadness for she knew it was probably the last time.

When Betty walked into the day room, she saw Louie and said, "Louie, I am so happy for you."

Louie smiled and hugged her then said, "Mrs. Payson, will you tell me one more story before I leave."

"Of course," Betty answered.

"Can we sit on our special bench?" Louie asked.

Betty quickly responded, "Yes, let's go."

It was a chilly but sunny day in Chicago. They each grabbed their jackets and snuggled up on their special bench. Betty began...

"One day I went down to the creek to get some water for my mom and on my way back a big black snake started to chase me......."

THE END

About the Author

Joyce Bennett-Hall lives in Southern California with her husband Shawn and their two dogs, Pablo and Tina. She has two adult children and two grandchildren. Joyce is an author, speaker, life coach, counselor and an ordained interfaith minister. Betty, is her third book and her first fiction novella. It is the first book in a trilogy.

Joyce's self-help book Deliberate Decisions, A Simple Guide for Real Success, came about from her experiences as a coach, counselor and minister. Joyce co-wrote the book Providence, A Story of Love, Hope and Diversity, a true story about Joyce and her husband Shawn.

Books by
Joyce Bennett-Hall

Books written by Joyce Bennett-Hall can be found by visiting her website, JoyceBennettHall.com and include:

Providence, A Story of Hope, Love and Diversity

Deliberate Decisions, A Simple Guide for Real Success

Betty, A Story of Big City Dreams